Prologue

Echoing across the vast swathes of farmed fenlanα, ιιι. -
that particular morning summoning the inhabitants of the village to church as they had for hundreds of years. A few, mainly older, inhabitants of the village obeyed their once imperious calls and straggled towards the church, unaware, as was the bell-ringer, that the summoning bell was the tolling bell too on this occasion, tolling for the passing for one of their own who now lay dead in the murky fenland waters, hidden by the undergrowth and soon to be food for the marauding wild life.
A young man who had once been brought to this church in his family's christening gown, held by a proud young mother, would never marry in its hallowed sanctums and it looked unlikely that he would be buried in the quiet churchyard where the rabbits were the bane of the elderly gardener. A mother would never hug her son again (although considering the son, it is doubtful whether his interactions with her included such pleasant physical contact. The bruises frequently visible on her arms, and presently around her neck, suggested a different story of physical contact).
Slowly, the parishioners headed up the path and entered the church where services had taken place for centuries. Inside the church, they took their accustomed pews and found their places in the service and hymn books, dog-eared from many years of use. Smilingly, they greeted each other, friends and neighbours of many years, family friends of generations in some cases. They rose as the vicar walked down the aisle and the service started just as every other day for as long as anyone could remember.
In a house in the village, a mother had left out breakfast before she went to church, in case her son came home for it, without any expectation of it being eaten when she returned , but because she thought that was what good mothers do. Meanwhile, she sat, head bowed in church, listening to the service unaware of her wayward son's fate.
Nearby, by another, far larger and modernised house, a young teenager was sullenly getting into the back seat of an expensive modern BMW seemingly oblivious to her surroundings, while a still-young-looking father got into the front with a look of relief. The boot held a couple of suitcases and anyone looking carefully would

see that under the sunglasses, the girl's eyes were red rimmed.
Without conversation, or even looking at each other, they departed.
In church, the vicar had reached his sermon. He prided himself on an interesting sermon. He tried so hard to not be too long-winded, academic or boring. He knew his flock would benefit from an understandable sermon rather than a show of his academic prowess and tried to deliver such. He spoke on the lesson of Jesus feeding the 5000, relating it to our modern day and how we as Christians could follow the example of Jesus. His parishioners listened, for the most part, intently. A bored child yawned and sighed from time to time. The vicar silently thanked Jesus for such a receptive and kind flock and asked for guidance in growing his flock as he spoke.
By the time the vicar had finished his sermon and moved onto the peace and communion, the BMW had returned to its neat driveway without the sullen teenager and a far more jaunty looking man than before climbed out of the car shouting cheery a greeting as he entered the house.
By the time he had finished a cup of coffee, the congregation were filing out of church and this Sunday resembled any other sunny weekend day with a flurry of car washing, children on bikes, gardening, washing being hung out and barbecues set up. The echoes of timelessness were lost and the fenland rang with the sounds of modern life.

Chapter 1

Arrival.

Briefly, as the car drove along, she looked up at her surroundings. It was too dark to really see where they were, somewhere in the countryside, somewhere flat. Drearily and uninterested, she stared unseeingly into the distance. Beside her, he drove on into the night, confident where he was going without comment. They sat silently together mainly, comfortable companionship on his side, oblivious to the sadness radiating from her.
She sat huddled, a woman of around thirty, long highlighted blonde hair loose around her, a pretty but modest summer dress (the type he approved of) and sandals on, a light cardigan held on her lap. On her left hand she wore a wedding ring, no longer shiny. Her face wore light make up, the type women know is there and men hail as natural beauty. Her resting face looked sad and she made no attempt to

interact with her companion.
In contrast, he sat with a jovial grin upon his slightly jowled face and occasionally reached over to pat her hand or point out a barely visible landmark. He radiated insincere bonhomie in his body language. You could imagine him hosting a party, welcoming his guests, sharing a beer or something stronger with his friends, accepting compliments for the wonderful house and party while behind him his wife scurried around providing the drinks, preparing the food and afterwards clearing up while he put his feet up exhausted by the party, chiding her gently for not being more sociable,for running out of a certain beverage, or for the money she had spent.
Soon, the silence bored him and he started talking to her, animatedly telling her about their destination. She sat, smiling gently at him, nodding and agreeing on autopilot when expected but the sadness never left her eyes.
'It is a beautiful house, an old pub originally, but closed now of course- couldn't see us running a pub- not lucrative these days!' He chuckled at his own wisdom. 'Closed over fifty years ago, so no need to worry some old timers will resent us for destroying the heart of the village, or anything like that! They wouldn't even have been old enough to drink at it! One of the front rooms was the bar, the bar is still in there, perfect for parties, I can see myself getting a barrel of beer and serving it at one of our parties. You will have to be more sociable though, get to know the neighbours, of course. It is a village, have to be part of village life, especially owning the old pub and all that. We'll have standing in the village with a house this size. Five bedrooms, en suite to ours of course, cant have people seeing you in your nightie the morning after a party, put their wives nose out of joint with you being so much younger and all... ' He looked across at her, as she mechanically smiled at his comment- compliment as he would see it. He squeezed her thigh, a bit higher than she liked, but she forced herself not to flinch but to continue smiling as he glanced at her before he continued. 'All five bedrooms are a decent size, large enough for a couple to stay in but the main bathroom is dated, but we can sort that when probate comes through, and landscape the garden, the patio is dated- eighties crazy paving, we'll get decking or sandstone with that money, and bifold doors and a gazebo with a hot tub in. Garden is lawn but I'm sure you can sort

flower beds and hanging baskets, it isn't like you have much else to do now we are out of London, away from your job and your Gran has gone.' Again he looked at her expecting her smiling agreement, but this time her face was turned away and he wasn't wily enough to check her reflection in the car window as she blinked back tears. Below her cardigan, her hands were balled up into fists with her nails digging into her palms, hard enough to hurt and mark with indented half moon shapes, but not hard enough to draw blood, he didn't like marks anyone- including himself- could see. It was the mention of probate, her Gran and the money he saw coming her way, he had already spent it in his head a few days after the funeral, without even asking her what she thought. Nothing new really.
'I've arranged for Pete and Gill- the Lancasters- to visit in the middle of August, so you will need to have everything unpacked and sorted by then.' Again he looked to her and she muttered agreement quietly.
' I'm thinking maybe we will try to get a couple more of the old crew up then too Mike and Kay, Andy and Linda, maybe Geoff and his wife- can't remember her name but you can look it up. Weather should be good for a barbecue, I'll be cooking so not too much pressure on you just the salads and desserts which won't take you a minute. You'll have to get to know some of the village- the right sort of course- so we can invite a few of them, make it a real occasion. You know the type I mean! Maybe there is a village vicar, that would look good.' He looked at her again expecting agreement and she nodded.
'Where exactly is our new house?' She asked quietly.
'It is a surprise. Beautiful house, you'll love it. Good job I drove your car up here a few days ago, bit hairy some of these lanes, don't want you driving around in the dark in that little car of yours. Maybe we will get you something bigger, a BMW maybe?' Had he been looking at her at this point, he would have seen a look of horror pass over her face. 'Or an Audi. Lots of Volvos up here, but they look a bit frumpy and that is something you are not, although I think you could do with joining a fitness class, I've noticed those abs aren't looking so honed these days.' he gently elbowed her, pleased at the joke he had just made at her expense. She smiled in the expected manner at him as he glanced at her. As his eyes returned to the road, her glance briefly dropped from his face to his once washboard stomach before returning unseeingly to the road ahead.

'Nearly there now, next town is Fenland Market and then we are only a few minutes away.' Had he been looking carefully at her, he'd have seen her face change and a brief look of pain come over her face before it returned to the blank mask of before. ' And now we have a big house in the country, maybe I will be more agreeable to that idea of babies you keep putting forth. After all, no job now, you need something to keep you busy.' again he glanced at her and she obediently smiled. 'I'm a lucky man to have a good wife like you. This will be a new start for us, we will be far happier here.'
This time she really did look happier. 'I hope so.' she replied, reaching her hand out briefly and stroking his arm.
Just then, he turned into a village and her brief look of horror when she saw the sign suggested that for her it wasn't quite the happy arrival he had envisaged.

Chapter 2

And she was fourteen again. Sitting sullenly in her Dad's new BMW as he told her what a wonderful summer they would have together. How much fun she would have with Sheryl, how Sheryl couldn't wait to see her but the morning sickness meant she couldn't cope with being in the car.
A year after her mum had died in a car crash on her way home from work, he had remarried. After the crash, she had been sent to live with her Gran, Mum's Mum. Kind, funny and loving. She had lived just around the corner and been part of their everyday life anyway, picking her up from school and looking after her until mum got home. Dad worked long hours, had trips away, it made sense. So she had moved into her Gran's house where she already had a bedroom next door to her Mum's childhood bedroom. It didn't make sense for Dad to keep an entire house and mortgage when it was just him, he downsized to a flat near his work and soon was too busy to pop in more than once a week, if he didn't have to travel.
Then, ten months after the crash, he came to pick them up for her birthday meal, her 14th birthday, with Sheryl. He worked with Sheryl and she had been so kind to him. He knew mum would want him to be happy. Soon her birthday meal had turned into their engagement meal and Gran was smilingly welcoming Sheryl to the family.
When they had emptied the house before Dad moved out, along with

her own things and Mum's jewellery and books, she had picked up her mother's diaries, going back years. She had been secretly reading them at night instead of the Sweet Valley High and Agatha Christie her Gran presumed she was rereading. Sheryl was mentioned in the last two diaries. It was a secret pain which she had no intention of inflicting on her Gran. But it hardly endeared Sheryl to her.
And now her Dad was bringing her to spend the summer with him, and Sheryl, who apparently was ill with morning sickness, whatever that was.
When her Dad married Sheryl, the flat he owned in London became too small, the area too dangerous, too congested, and they had sold it, using the money to buy a house out of London where prices were cheaper, a house in the countryside, big, with a garden where Sheryl planned to grow her own vegetables. The weekly visits had become fortnightly as it was such a long way. Then he announced on the last visit that she was coming to stay with them for the summer. It was clear that neither her nor Gran had a say in whether this happened. After all, he was her only parent.
She had made plans for the summer with her friends. Plans to go swimming, shopping, have sleepovers, go to see her Gran's sister (Auntie Elinor) who had a Pekinese and three budgies. But her plans were swept aside without a hearing as her father put his foot down and uttered ominous words about family, duty, discipline and step mother. With a sinking heart, she wordlessly smiled accepting this was now her fate. She knew not to try to argue. Her mother had instilled that in her when she was very young. At least, come September, she would be back in London with her Gran and her friends.
And she was sure Sheryl wouldn't be the wicked step mother of the fairytales, well she really hoped not. Her friend Emmie had a stepmother and she was really fun. She bought Emmie a cropped Adidas t shirt that her mum would never let her wear and gave her half a glass of wine when she opened a bottle on nights her Dad was out. Maybe Sheryl would be like that? Although she didn't like wine, Gran had let her try a sip last New Year's Eve, her nose curled at the memory of the sour taste.
She decided to really give it a chance, mum wouldn't have wanted her to be bitter. She obviously didn't want her to know about Sheryl otherwise she would have told her rather than writing it in her diary

on a page with water splats, hidden in her locked bookcase. She only had her Dad and Gran left now. Her dad clearly had no idea her mum wrote diaries, let alone that she hid them there as he wouldn't have wanted her to read those either. Sheryl hadn't been the first name in the book. Marie, Lisa and Joanne all featured in previous years starting when Mum had been pregnant with her. Like Gran, Mum had been a good Catholic who believed in her marriage vows. Marriage vows were sacred, that had been taught from an early age, and men had pressures and temptations women didn't. Wives should support their husbands, and children must honour their parents.
She had wondered once how as good Catholics both her and her Mum had been only children. A look at her Grandfather's gravestone next to her Mum's in the graveyard had confirmed her Gran had not had the chance to have more children as her husband had died the same year her mother was born. When she started her periods a few months ago, she realised she had never in her childhood seen the evidence of her mother having them and her Gran had confirmed her mother had had to have a hysterectomy after the difficult birth with her.
She looked out at the flat landscape around her, it reminded her of the Little House on the Prairie episodes she had watched on TV. So flat, fields that seemed to go on forever and sky larger and wider than she had ever seen. The villages they had passed through seemed so insignificant compared to the London she was used to or the busy tourist resorts they had visited in the summers. She hoped they were at least going to be in a town. She hoped it wasn't going to be too lonely a summer.
Her Dad suddenly called her to attention and pointed out local landmarks, Fenland Market they were passing, the nearest town to the village which would be her home this summer. Just a few more minutes before they were there, minutes he filled with explanations of the local farming crop- sugar beet – which would be harvested in autumn and winter and taken to the factory whose chimneys were just visible on the horizon. With a sinking feeling she looked at the small village they were driving into which he pointed out as their new home.

Chapter 3

The familiar feeling of dread landed in her stomach as they turned into the village. There wasn't really enough light to see if it had changed much. The shadows looked familiar, but not in a comforting way, it felt oppressive. She swallowed the desire to scream and composed her face.
Her heart was beating wildly in her chest, it sounded so loud to her she was amazed he couldn't hear it and wasn't commenting on it. She felt bile rising in her throat and the bitter taste in her mouth. She hastily drank a few sips of water so he wouldn't be able to smell or taste it on her. Sickness in the car was viewed as a negative reflection on his driving and she could neither explain or cope with the small digs and moodiness she would have to endure. She felt the sweat on her hands and wiped them surreptitiously on her cardigan. A line from Casablanca jumped into her head, 'Of all the Gin Joints in all the towns in the world, she walks into mine.' Except this wasn't a Gin Joint, it was the village that she had hoped to never return to. Her husband had begun talking to her again, she tried to shut out the tendrils of the past and concentrate on the present, and on him.
' The people who owned it before us had it for about five years, they started renovating it- modernised the main bedroom -thankfully- looking at the state of the bathroom it can't have been very modern before – and they did a great job with the kitchen and two family rooms. There is room downstairs I will make my den- I'll put a surround sound system in there and I suppose your books and computer had better go in the smallest of the upstairs bedrooms- they used it as a linen closet so there is no heating in that one but I'm sure you will be fine in there. It isn't as if you really need to spend much time in it, I know you planned to work from home but it really would look better if you didn't. See what the other women in the village do and join in their coffee mornings, sewing clubs or whatever women do. Just pulling up now- wait in the car and I will come round and open the door, I will carry you over the threshold too- got to give the right impression. And for god sake look a little happier, I've bought a beautiful house for you, look grateful.' The last was whisper shouted at her.
He pulled up on a large gravel driveway in front of a large double fronted red brick building and once again she felt the feeling of dread in her stomach. The arm of coincidence truly was long! She felt her car door opening beside her and carefully schooled her face

into a look of delight as she took his hand and exited the car, her cardigan held tightly in one hand with white knuckles. She could see curtains in a couple of nearby houses moving and guessed they were being watched.
He leaned forward to kiss her passionately and she responded willingly. He made his kiss long and passionate and she knew he too had seen the curtains moving in the nearby windows. He pulled her towards the door, a wide smile on his face, unlocked it and swept her into his arms, his muscular six foot body easily lifting her five foot slim frame from the floor and holding her in an embrace that looked loving and romantic for the watchers. He carried her over the threshold, his lips on hers again and entered the house, kicking the door closed behind him.
Immediately, he put her down and fumbled for the light switch. He walked through the hall past the oak doors which she knew well and had led to the two front rooms and past the doors which had led to the kitchen and study on each side and to a door at the back of the house which had not previously been there. This led to a huge kitchen, diner, family room, a new addition presumably added by the previous residents who had improved the house.
All their furniture from the downstairs of their house in London had been put in this room, and it left room to spare! At one end was a kitchen fitted in the shaker country style, cream wooden units, a Belfast sink and built in appliances. Opening a drawer, she could see the movers he had hired had even unpacked their kitchen equipment into convenient places. On the other side of an island,which doubled as a breakfast bar, was their pine table and chairs, with the extra leaf put in it to try to fill the space and the large corner sofa and coffee table. These which had filled the living room of their London terraced house seemed smaller in this huge room. Double glass doors- presumably the ones he wanted to replace with bifold doors – opened to outside, to where she remembered a rough lawn and paddock behind with a gate to the footpath behind the village. It was too dark to see how that had changed.
It really was a beautiful room. She smiled at him gratefully and said,'Thank you for all this, it is beautiful.' He smiled back at her and she hoped in her heart that they could be happy, like they used to be, before. They could have a new start, together.
He flopped onto their comfortable sofa. 'Long drive,' he said, 'I could

murder a coffee.'
Immediately, she nodded and went to find the items she needed in the new kitchen. By the time she had made him a coffee and a herbal tea for herself he was asleep on the sofa, snoring gently. She sat down beside him on the sofa, placing the drinks on the coffee table and he roused sufficiently to pull her towards him in a one armed embrace before recommencing snoring. With a sigh of satisfaction, she rested her head on his shoulder and closed her eyes.
They could be happy together again here, like they used to be? Her Gran had always said it took effort and pain to make a marriage work. She wasn't shy of putting in the effort.

Chapter 4

The house her Dad and Sheryl (she couldn't bring herself to call a woman the same age as her friend Katie's sister, step-mother, or even think it) had bought looked like it was an old house that had been made more modern. The front of the house had a plastic porch on it and the windows on each side of the door and above were shiny white PVC and plastic, there were net curtains at the windows, shrouding the inside in privacy. What had probably once been a front garden was now gravel able to park far more cars than just Sheryl's RAV4 and her Dad's new BMW. There was a large bracket on the wall at almost roof level above the front door, it looked as though something should be hanging from it, but it was far too high for a hanging basket (two of those adorned the wall on either side of the front door, with pink and purple fuscias spilling over the sides of the baskets).
Her father went ahead of her and opened the porch door and the white plastic and stained glass door depicting a very improbable rose and lily pattern before they entered a wide hallway.
'Sweetheart, I'm home.' Her Dad called out with the same over-cheerful voice he had been using with her in the car.
Following the sound, her dad led her into a very white room, white walls, ceilings, sofa, coffee table and armchair. Even the television unit was white. Only the TV with it's grey and brown frame was familiar, and not white. Lying across the sofa, was Sheryl.
'Still feeling rough? Don't you worry now, we are here now and we will look after you, won't we?' He said with a frown at his daughter. 'No need for you to lift a finger, while you have us here. You just

concentrate on growing that little tyke.' He nodded down at the flat stomach Sheryl was still sporting, and they both looked towards his daughter.
Her mouth dropped open as she realised the relevance of morning sickness and the phrase 'little tyke' Sheryl was pregnant. Sheryl and Dad were having a baby. She hadn't really known anyone pregnant before, except a couple of teachers and they didn't talk to the girls at her Catholic girls' school about things like that, so she hadn't thought anything of the phrase in the car, but now she remembered pregnant women were sometimes sick. She realised Sheryl was talking and she had missed most of what she was saying.
'...of course you would want to be here to get to know your little brother- I just know it will be a boy- and your Dad would really like a boy, after all he already has one girl and your mum didn't give him a son, every man wants a son. And I've been so sick, poor Tom-Tom is so busy with work, it wasn't really fair to expect him to look after me but he knew you would want to do it. After all, you are fifteen now and it must be so boring stuck in that awful old house with your old Gran and all that dreary Catholic religion. Far more fun for you to be here helping your dad and me with things in this nice modern house. All the cleaning to keep it nice is far too hard in my condition and we knew you had nothing better to do.'
She listened to the end of Sheryl's speech and realised she was there to do the housework and make their life easier, she wasn't really wanted. And she would far rather be at Gran's house with her friends popping in and her Gran planning day trips and sharing her interests with her. She realised both her Dad (or Tom-Tom as Sheryl had called him) and Sheryl were staring at her expectantly.
'Aren't you going to congratulate us?' Her dad asked.
In a flurry hiding her internal numbness, she smiled, hugged them both and uttered what she hoped sounded like heartfelt congratulations, she looked carefully at her dad to make sure she didn't see the slight narrowing of his eyes that usually signified she had disappointed him. All seemed well and Sheryl continued explaining what was to happen while her father returned to the car for her two suitcases.
'...four bedrooms but five really, we have the largest bedroom, it even has an en-suite, the second and third bedroom are nearly as large, I'm making one of them into a nursery but it still needs

painting, you'll be able to help me with that, paint fumes aren't good for pregnant women and I'm sure you will want to do it. The other is a spare room for visitors, my parents pop down most weekends. The fourth bedroom Tom-Tom has made into a study for himself. But don't worry there is another little room- the estate agent called it a dressing room because it is a bit small, we have made it into a bedroom for you, it fits a small single bed and a bedside cabinet in. There is a chest of drawers in the hall you can use. I know you will love being here with us. Far more fun than with your fusty old gran!'
She smiled mechanically and nodded at intervals in Sheryl's speech before she heard her dad calling her and excused herself to go upstairs where he was calling her from.
The stairs were also painted white, as was the hallway, and when she got there, the landing too. She ascended the staircase and joined her father outside a white door.
'So this is your bedroom,' he announced, flinging open a white door to a carpeted white room. The bed frame and bedside cabinet (which were all the furniture that could fit in the room) were white, the quilt and curtains however were a light green- her favourite colour- she felt hopeful that maybe her dad wanted her there as more than a helper for her Sheryl.
She turned to him, 'Green, thank you Dad, my favourite colour, I'm so pleased you remembered.' She smiled at him and put her arms out to hug him.
After awkwardly accepting the hug, he pointed out the chest of drawers in the hallway she could unpack her clothes into and the shelves high on the wall above her bed where she could store her books. He also pointed out the bathroom, down the corridor (which had obviously been decorated before Sheryl and him had moved in as it held a pink suite, pink tiles and a beige coloured lino floor). There was an empty shelf in the cupboard there for her to store her toiletries. He left her to unpack, and headed back down the stairs.

Chapter 5

The upstairs looked the same at first glance, two double bedrooms at the front of the house with the small room or large cupboard which had once been her bedroom (and was now to be her unheated office) between them. The door which led to the family bathroom- she

grinned wryly when opening it to find the same pink bathroom suite and tiles her dad and Sheryl had hated so many years before- was still in the same place and inside only the flooring had changed to a more modern (still cream) vinyl floor. At the back of the house, there was a change however, instead of three doors, there was one to a bedroom she remembered as having been the main bedroom with an advocado en suite, (which seemed to have vanished) and a corridor leading to two further bedrooms over the kitchen extension. One was another double, and the final one a huge master suite with walk in wardrobes and an en suite bathroom.
Her husband was so proud of the house he had bought without consulting her and moved their belongings to while she had been nursing her Gran. His enthusiasm was infectious, and so, rarely for her these days, she found herself smiling widely and enjoying seeing him transform back into the enthusiastic, affectionate man she had married a decade ago.
'The people we bought from said a previous owner had painted the entire house white! Woodwork, walls, ceilings etc. The carpets were white and even the windows were white PVC. They went for a much more cottagey feel to the place and I really like it. Apparently, they had even put a white PVC porch on! What sort of vandal does that to a lovely period piece like this?'
For a brief moment she imagined saying, 'My dad.' and imagining his reaction. But before the thought could take full root in her head, he had continued.
'The main bathroom is dire, early 90s I believe, but the last owners were a couple and used their en suite, didn't see the need to replace it, functional for the occasional guest, just dated. We will of course change that soon. Downstairs is a shower room, so no reason for us to use it, and when probate comes through we can sell your gran's old place and modernise as I was saying about earlier...'
He continued, without even noticing the frown on her face. She didn't want to sell her gran's house. It was her home in a way no where else ever had been and as inheritance was her personal property, not an asset of their marriage (as per the prenuptial contract he had her sign. At a time she hadn't finished university and he had far greater assets than her, having a job and holding a mortgage on the one bedroom flat they had started their marriage in. He had also had high hopes for inheriting his grandparent's home upon their

death, as the only grandson, it had turned out his grandparents weren't quite as dismissive of the claims of their three children and four granddaughters as he was). When the pre-nup (as he called it) was mentioned these days by him, it was with suggestions of overturning it. Privately, she had no plans of doing so- or of selling her gran's terraced house in a busy London suburb, but that was a discussion for another day.
As he had been talking, he had been leading her around the upstairs of their new house, he had now led them back to the main bedroom, their bedroom.
'Of course I asked the movers to organise the kitchen, I needed to use that, but I didn't fancy the idea of someone poking around our personal items so our clothes are still packed in suitcases in the walk in wardrobe- I just unpacked myself a few necessities. The same in the bathroom, in our vanity cases apart from a few of my essentials. I will leave you to unpack in the week while I'm at work. I made up the bed of course, had to sleep somewhere, so let's just get to bed tonight and sort things out tomorrow.'
'Oh yes, I'm so tired, and you were driving so must be even more so. I will have a shower and we will go to bed. Thank you so much for organising all this.'
He left her to organise herself and disappeared back into the bedroom. Within fifteen minutes, she joined him in the huge king-size bed. He was lying on his back, reading glasses on, holding his phone in front of him. She leaned over to kiss him goodnight and he snatched his phone out of her line of vision before replying with a reluctant lukewarm kiss. She turned off her side light and heart - sinking turned to face him. She wanted to ask him so many questions but knew better than to do so. He too turned, his body away from her and phone held low in front of him to make sure she could not see it. She felt disappointed and the loneliness which always seemed to be there these days, bubbled up to the surface. She felt tears pricking her eyes and quickly blinked them away in case he turned back.
A few moments later, he put his phone down and turned back towards her.
'An e mail from work, had to answer it. Confidential and all.' he said. She wanted so much to believe him completely as she always used to, but the shadow of doubt remained. She smiled brightly despite the doubt and feeling in the pit of her stomach and he leaned towards

her kissing her and touching her.
Once again, happiness and hope rose in her and she pressed her body against his lost in the love she felt for him. Of course it was work, she was being ridiculous.
His arms came around her, holding her tightly and as she always had, she felt so safe in his arms. She wrapped her arms around him and kissed him, feeling his hands loosen from around her and one hand cup her buttocks and roughly pull her tighter towards his body.
An hour later, he lay sleeping beside her, her head on his shoulder as she felt the rise and fall of his breathing beside her.
'I love you.' she whispered but he was fast asleep and could not reply and somehow, she realised she wouldn't necessarily believe him completely anyway.

Chapter 6
Her first night had started so differently all those years ago. After clearing up from the dinner she had 'helped' Sheryl to cook, as Sheryl was far too tired after all the cooking she had (or hadn't) done, she was then told to go upstairs to read in her room as they needed some quiet adult time. Door closed, she had lain on her bed and read Venetia by Georgette Heyer. She read it every summer, as did Gran. Sometimes they read their favourite bits to each other and they often quoted bits at each other. A summer idyll in the countryside, where the young beautiful maiden meets the charming rake, Damerel, a romance filled with classical quotes and stolen kisses ensues. Who wouldn't want to meet their own lord Damerel?
Halfway through the book she heard footsteps and giggles, she realised her dad and Sheryl were going to bed, so turned out her light to avoid being told to. The travel clock she had put on her bedside cabinet showed 10pm, so she thought she may as well try to sleep.
Lying in bed, under her quilt she closed her eyes and listened to the sounds of the occasional car and the wildlife outside. Then, with the next sounds, she opened her eyes in the horror of all children ever realising what is happening in their parents' rooms.
First there were hushed giggles and the occasional squeak from the bed, the squeaking quickly became more rhythmical and the giggles and exclamations less hushed.
'Ohhhh Tom-Tom, like that, yes, there, ooh harder, harder...'
'Grrrr oooh, yes, mmmm.'

'yes, yes, uh,uh, UHHHHH!'
Even hands over her ears seemed to make no difference. For the first time since her fourteenth birthday, she felt the tears pricking in her eyes overflow and tried to stay silent as sobs wracked her body. She just wanted to go home, to be in her bedroom, with gran snoring gently in the room below her and the familiar pictures on the wall. She didn't want to be here, with them. She hadn't realised until tonight how much she depended on Gran. Since Mum had gone (she couldn't bring herself to use the word died, it sounded so stark, cold and final), Gran was the person she knew she could always rely on, whatever. Gran had always been there, alongside Mum, then later just Gran. Dad had always been busy with work, around less often, dashing out evenings after getting home from work and preoccupied when he was home. But for the first time ever, Gran wasn't nearby. Even after the squeaking and muffled cries were over, she could still hear them in her mind. She felt, unfairly maybe, that the cries which were all Sheryl, were done on purpose to remind her she wasn't really wanted. Until she could be useful, there had been no visits to this house they shared. She was only here to be useful.
She lay, unsleeping, in her bed for what felt like hours. The room was hot, the window seemed to be locked and she could not locate a key. Eventually, she decided to go downstairs and get a glass of water to quench her thirst. Slowly, feeling her way, she crept down the stairs and stood in the small white kitchen drinking a glass of water. It was cool down here, far cooler than her bedroom. She refilled her glass of water and noticed a board with keys on hooks. She turned on the lights and located one labelled upstairs study window key. Taking it, and her glass of water, with her, she headed slowly back up the stairs to bed.
Window opened and a cool breeze blowing through, the room felt much more comfortable and she lay in bed daydreaming of dangerous older men like Damerel, ready to sweep her off her feet in a haze of poetry and literary quotations, interspersed (of course) with passionate kissing. She wasn't really so sure about what happened after, but that was only after marriage, part of the price for a happily ever after?
She had never kissed a boy. She was fifteen, sixteen very soon, and some of her friends had kissed boys. But attending a girls' catholic school and being brought up by a gran who was a pillar of the local

Catholic church didn't really give many opportunities for meeting males who wanted to so much as discuss Greek mythology or quote restoration poetry at you. The only boys she knew from church had been annoying children who pulled her hair and called her smelly and now ignored her to play football or go off together as the boys could while the girls 'helped' the women.
She had read all about kissing in Sweet Valley High, they had all read them from first to third year although she didn't think Gran had been very impressed by the one she had flicked through. She had wanted to be just like Elizabeth Wakefield, beautiful and clever. She had realised, just clever would have to do. Her hair was a boring brown that fell to her waist. It would still be neatly plaited in two plaits if her gran had her way, but she had rebelled and insisted on wearing it in a ponytail. It got more knots but she thought at least she looked older than with two plaits. She was short, six inches shorter than Elizabeth Wakefield's five foot six inches, and her eyes were boring brown rather than hazel, blue or green. She was skinny and her breasts hadn't really grown until this year. Now they had, nothing seemed to fit her properly. Venetia was beautiful and clever too, another tall blonde girl whose clothes fitted perfectly and who was a sportswoman whereas she was always the last to be picked for team sports. No wonder they got the Todds and Damerels of this world.
She lay in bed conjuring situations where an older boy- a man- would see her and recognise some beauty in her, not just in her looks but in her soul. Would find her irresistible and befriend her in her loneliness, sharing his worldly knowledge and loving her. He would be tall, not that it was hard to be tall compared to her, with dark hair worn in disarray (as Heyer's heroes frequently had). He would have piercing blue eyes, and a be good looking and strong. And a man like that would never fall in love with her...
She turned over and closed her eyes trying to get her unlikely hero to vanish so she could fall asleep. After all, even if he existed, what was the chance of meeting him in this tiny village? No chance! Although honestly, should any boy approach her, she would have no idea what to say and would probably be so embarrassed she would try to escape. Probably a lucky escape for the Damerels of this world.
She lay lonely and discontented in bed for a while until sleep overcame her and she knew nothing more until the morning.

Chapter 7

The morning arrived all too soon. Always a light sleeper, she was awoken by the church summoning bell and turned over to look at her still sleeping husband. This used to be her favourite time in the morning, awake before him, encircled in his arms feeling the warmth of his body against hers and listening to him breathe. As he woke up, he used to pull her closer and kiss her. Nowadays, she woke to his back and should she cuddle up to him, he would move away. There seemed little point staying in bed, so she quietly got up and went to start her day.

Before going downstairs, she went to look at her new study, her bedroom all those years ago. There was no bed in it now, just a desk and chair which had been in their old house and four large boxes on the floor containing her computer and things she needed for the job she loved and her husband was so keen for her to leave. She knew she had no plans to leave it and felt guilty for her determination to carry on against his wishes. Part of her she was sure her Mum and Gran would both have been horrified by her disobeying the husband she had promised to 'love honour and obey', but surely they would have understood that without them there to shield her she needed the security of being able to earn her own living. Incase, like Gran, she became a widow unexpectedly (or he left her for another woman, one who would be a better wife for him).

'Always be independent, darling. Keep a savings and current account in your own name, however much you trust them. If they truly love you, they will want you to have that.' She could hear Gran saying that as if it was yesterday. She knew from reading Mum's diary that she had kept her own accounts, and had been glad she did when their joint accounts were suddenly suspiciously short of money and Dad had been home less and less. She also knew that Gran had not just told Mum to do that but made it a condition of her marriage to Dad. Except the savings account hadn't just been in her Mum's name, it had been jointly in her Gran's name and her name. And thanks to Gran's saving, there was a considerable amount in there which she had not known about until after her Gran's death, large enough that she had no fears of not being able to pay the bills on Gran's house whether or not she was working. Her fears of disappointing her Mum and Gran disappeared. While they had believed in marriage and

being guided by their husbands, they had also believed a woman needed money to fall back on, just in case, and for both of them that money had been a godsend.
She suddenly realised that she had become a wife who hid things from her husband. She hadn't used to be that way. A year ago, she would have immediately told him about the money in that bank account, and the shares in her name, and Gran's house being jointly in her name. But now, it seemed wiser not to. Her trust had been eroded and she couldn't be certain any longer, and a part of her didn't really know how she wanted her future to be if she couldn't have things how they were before.
She walked into the kitchen, and automatically put the coffee machine on and pulled out two cups. Then a strange look came over her face for a moment and she turned the kettle on. A quick look in cupboards found tea bags and she made a cup of tea, leaving the coffee in the pot to stay warm.
Leaving the cup of tea to cool, she decided to look around the rest of the downstairs. The front two rooms, she knew would be devoid of furniture. She walked into the room to the left of the front door, which had been a dining room once. It was empty of furniture but the once boarded over fireplace had been opened up and a large wood burner sat there. She made a mental note to organise a chimney sweep, logs, firelighters and fire tools. It would make a lovely living room, cosy in the winter and with the sash windows flung open, airy in the summer. The room to the right of the front door contained a surprise. Previously this had been a sitting room, but where the sofa had once sat was now a large antique looking wooden bar. To anyone who hadn't previously known the house, it would seem the original bar from when it had been a pub was still in situ, but she knew well it had not been there fifteen years ago and instead the then dining room had held a hatch through from the kitchen where beer had originally been served. Both rooms needed furnishing, their small London Terraced house had not held enough furniture to furnish a large house like this.
Behind the now bar room was a shower room and utility room. Opposite was a small study (previously the kitchen) which her husband- who did not work from home- had clearly decided was his. She noted it was heated and decided if she was to work upstairs she would need some sort of heater for the room in Winter. All in all, it

looked as though he had left the job of furnishing the rooms to her- but to his tastes of course.
She returned to the kitchen and poured his coffee. Slowly and carefully, she made her way upstairs carrying his coffee to place beside him for when he woke up. She then made her way into their walk in wardrobe and started to unpack some clothes of hers so she could shower and dress. As she was about to enter the shower, she heard the sounds of her husband waking and decided to leave him undisturbed while she took her shower.
After showering and dressing, she re-entered the bedroom to find him sitting in bed on his phone, the coffee half-drunk beside him. As soon as heard her enter the room, the smile fell slightly from his face and he held his phone closer.
'Good Morning Darling,' she said leaning in for a kiss. 'Do we have any plans today?'
'I thought we could go out for Sunday lunch, somewhere local. No pub in this village, but there is one in the next village. And shopping, you will need to go shopping, I got some basics in but now you are here, we will need some proper food for you to cook. Maybe a walk around the village, try to bump into some neighbours. Show ourselves a bit. You'll need to change into something a bit more country.'
She looked perplexed for a moment, she didn't really think she had anything that looked country, London life hadn't really demanded it. She was in jeans and a fitted t shirt, she could wear trainers, but she had a feeling that wasn't what he meant. She was about to disappoint him again. She shrank inwardly.
He seemed to sense her concern. 'Do you not have anything country?' He asked, his face creasing into a frown?
'I d-d-d-on't think so. Would you like to look, I can finish unpacking my clothes while you shower and then change into what you think best?' Fear filled her stomach.
'So you'll unpack *your* clothes? All your clothes, but not any of mine?'
'I'll do yours first if you prefer?' She was floundering, she knew she had said the wrong thing.
He didn't bother to answer her, getting up and taking his phone with him through the walk in wardrobe and into the bathroom.
Shaking, she entered the walk-in wardrobe and started unpacking his

clothing, she had nearly finished, when he appeared naked looking for clothes for the day.
'You haven't changed yet?' He asked, his mouth pressed together in displeasure. He selected a pair of jeans and a t shirt along with underwear before returning to the bathroom where his phone was bleeping insistently.

Chapter 8

The first morning started promisingly. Sheryl and Dad seemed to be cheerful when they came downstairs. They had said last night to make her own breakfast, which she had, but she had also washed up after herself and their glasses and mugs from the previous night. They had no plans that morning and told her she should get to know the village, find some other children to play with. She had found herself shooed out the house like an unwanted cat, but that was infinitely better than sitting in the house uncomfortable with Dad and Sheryl. She was very glad she had had the forethought to grab a couple of books to read, as she was pretty sure any fellow fifteen year olds she saw were not going to want to incorporate her into their activities as six or ten year olds automatically did.
She decided as she had three hours to kill before lunch, she would walk around the village first, obeying her Dad's orders to get to know her surroundings, before finding somewhere quiet she could sit and read. The village looked as though it had one main road with a few smaller roads – cul de sacs mainly- branching off of it.
The main road was around half a mile long and she counted six small cul de sacs off of it. There was no pub or shop. The school looked closed and dilapidated with what had once been the playground tarmac looking bumpy and blistered with weeds growing through cracks. There was a park with a few swings, a slide and climbing frame and a large green area with goals where a group of boys who looked to be between eight and adult age were playing football. A collection of bikes were dumped at one side of the field. There were lots of houses, some big and posh looking, some small but neat looking and a couple that looked as though they needed some work done.
Outside lots of houses were cars with men washing them and TVs or radios could be heard through the open front doors. A few people

called a polite greeting as she walked past them and she tried hard to answer them, but as a Londoner greeting strangers did not come easily. There was a church which looked old and a graveyard which looked very neat and a field with two horses in. She stopped for a moment to admire the horses and noticed two girls about her age feeding them over the fence. She smiled nervously at them, but they giggled and looked away. Feeling like an intruder, she kept walking. She looked at her watch and there were still two and a half hours before she could go home. She wasn't a stupid child, she had known very well that her Dad's firm 'And you can stay out until 12.30pm.' meant don't come home and bother us until 12.30pm. She had thought of trying to find a secluded area to sit and read in the graveyard but she noticed a young man, only a few years older than herself, walking down a narrow path marked footpath. As the idea of sitting among gravestones in a graveyard didn't really appeal, she thought she would wait, give him a good head start so he didn't see her (and she didn't have to uncomfortably greet any more strangers) and see what the footpath led to (and if there was a secluded nook she could sit with a book).

The footpath led through a farm first, between large barns and parked tractors, then past fields of something green. As a city girl, she wouldn't even pretend she had any idea what it was. And then the scenery changed, the ploughed fields on either side became rough woodland and the verges were no longer mowed. The verges were full of long grasses and wild flowers which she was sure had been in the Flower Fairy books and pictures at home which had originally been her Gran's when she was young and had delighted three generations now. Had she been younger, she would have held her breathe hoping to see fairies among the flowers as the girls in Cottingley had caught on camera. She recognised a foxglove with bee on it and in her head could hear Gran reading The Foxglove Fairy to her with mum beside them. Her chest ached and she longed to be little and feel safe with her Mum and Gran around her instead of unwanted here. Yarrow she recognised too, and then, hidden in the woodland, she spied a pond and a not very well worn path leading to it.

Following the path through the wood- a forest in her mind, she tried to avoid stinging nettles and brambles, she felt glad of her jeans and trainers now, although she had wondered if it would be too hot in them, but the woodland was so much cooler and breezier that if anything she wished her t shirt had long sleeves. She found a convenient log beside the water's edge and sat down. A look at her watch confirmed it was only 10.10am and no more than a fifteen minute walk home, so she had plenty of time to read. She looked at the books she had picked up at random from her pile (she had purposefully left Venetia at home, knowing Gran would also be reading it, she had decided to keep it as a bedtime read to comfort her and make her feel as though Gran was close, or at least linked to her in some untangible way). The Chalet School in Exile, an old favourite. She tended to read the Chalet School books secretly as she was 'too old' for them now, but how could you outgrow a book like that? At the very least it was a familiar comfort to read, but really it had everything in, drawing the line between good and evil, love, friendship, children in situations they didn't understand, loss, leaving a beloved place and starting anew. It was no wonder that this should appeal to her with her life experiences. It was ironic that the part of the book appealed least to her when she had first read it- the romance between Jo and Jack, should now be one of the most appealing parts. The romance of having someone you could depend on, who would love and care for you appealed to her loneliness. The other book was an Agatha Christie she had received for her birthday but not read yet, a nice easy read for a day like today. The Murder at the Vicarage. She had of course seen the Joan Hickson TV adaption, but the books were always better. She did like Miss Marple, the little old lady who knitted and listened and reminded her of Gran, so clever at understanding people. She opened that book and started reading.

Chapter 9

Ten minutes later, only one bag unpacked, she walked downstairs nervously wearing the same pair of jeans with wedge sandals and a flowery top. She could hear him in the kitchen so taking a breath she walked in with a smile on her face. He briefly glanced at her before returning his eyes to the coffee he had just made. He had made no comment on her clothing and she inwardly debated if she should ask him if he was happy with her outfit, but he hated her showing signs of insecurity, and would be annoyed for the rest of the day. On the other hand, if he didn't feel she had made enough effort, she would

also receive that treatment. With relief she noticed he hadn't made her a coffee and got herself a glass of water. She also noticed he was using a different cup to the one she had given him earlier and that it wasn't in the sink or dishwasher. She placed her half finished glass of water and headed upstairs to collect his cup.
Re-entering the room with his half finished coffee mug from earlier, she was relieved to see a smile on his face.
'I knew you'd find something suitable.' he commented as she rinsed out his cup from earlier and placed it in the dishwasher. 'We'll go for a walk before lunch and introduce ourselves to the neighbours.' he said as he left the room to get ready, leaving his used cup on the kitchen island he had been standing at. Quickly, she picked up the mug, rinsed it and placed it in the dishwasher before going to the front door to meet him.
Together they walked out the door, and he walked her towards the house next door, a tidy looking 1930s detached house. In the garden was a middle-aged lady dead heading some rambling pink roses which were trailing up trellises and around a decorative archway. Seeing them coming towards her, she waved an arm before removing gardening gloves and placing them in the trug beside her. She walked up to meet them.
'Ahh, you must be the Grangers, how lovely to meet you both. I've seen all the comings and goings of cars and trucks moving you in, and I saw you arrive last night. So romantic the way you carried her over the threshold, my Sam did that when we first bought this house, thirty years ago now. It was so exciting to have a home of our own! I presume this is your first home? Newly-weds?' She paused briefly in her monologue but before they could answer her, she continued, 'Anyway, you must come in for a drink, coffee, tea or something cold? I have some elderflower cordial if you would like it?'
This time, before she could continue, James answered, 'That would be lovely, I'm a coffee man myself but I'm sure my wife would love to try your elderflower cordial. So kind of you to assume we are newly-wed, but in fact we have been married for nearly ten years now. You know our name, but we don't know yours yet Mrs...' He left her title hanging in the air, for her to finish.
' Foreman, my Sam, Mr Foreman is inside, he was just winding the grandfather clock, he usually does it on a Saturday night, but he had an emergency operation last night and it was late when he got home

so he is doing it now. They only last eight days before stopping you know, quite annoying if you forget.
'An emergency operation? I'm so sorry, surely he won't want guests after that. Do you need anything?' She spoke kindly, feeling terrible for having intruded at such a time.
Mrs Foreman looked surprised then giggled, 'He is the surgeon dear, no surgery was done to him, he was the one doing it!' She held the door open for them and they entered a large farmhouse style kitchen, with units around the side and a wooden table and chairs in the centre. Just closing a clock door on one side was a middle aged gentleman. ' Our new neighbours, the Grangers, my dear.'
'Dr Foreman,' he said formally holding out his hand to the doctor. 'I'm Mr Granger and this is my wife, Mrs Granger.'
'Not Dr Foreman, Mr, us surgeons go by Mr. Dr Foreman is my wife, she is a paediatrician. Anyway, not so much of this formality, I'm Sam and Dr Foreman there is Sandy.'
''James, he said, holding his hand out.
In the meantime the two women were talking quietly and left the kitchen.
'We will go and sit in the living room and leave them to chat there, Sam will bring us through drinks in a moment. Do you like flowers, I love gardening, I find it so relaxing after the stress of the hospital?' Dr Foreman asked.
'Ive always lived in London,' she answered, still amazed at the dynamics of a household where the husband would make and deliver drinks, that was definitely her job and had been her mother's too. She must ask Gran who had made the... and then it hit her again, that she could never ask Gran anything ever again. She realised she had paused speaking and tried very hard to continue the sentence she had started. 'And we never really had large gardens. The garden in my first childhood home was tiny and paved, more of a courtyard. Gran's had a lawn, fruit trees and soft fruits and our previous house just had a small patio area. I haven't really looked at the garden here, only a glance out the back door this morning, so I haven't really thought about the possibilities. I believe James would like a patio for entertaining.'
'Did you not come and see the house before you bought it?' Sandy asked in astonishment.
'No, we had put ours on the market when my gran became very ill, I

wasn't able to leave her, so when we had an offer on our house, James did everything. He wanted it to be a surprise for me.'
'And I hope you being here now means your gran has quite recovered?'
Tears pricked her eyes and she looked down as she replied mechanichally , 'She will never be ill or in pain again.' Somehow she couldn't bring herself to say the word dead and found herself repeating the words her gran had used to comfort her when her mum had died.
Sandy leaned forward and held her arm lightly for a moment. 'It is hard to lose those we love.' She said before changing the subject. Do you know this area at all? She asked, clearly trying to move onto a more neutral subject.
Choosing her words carefully, she replied, 'Not really, I've always lived in London. This will be a real change. I look forward to learning more about the area. You said that you've lived her thirty years? You must have seen a lot of change in the village?' As she looked at her smiling neighbour and she remembered her from fifteen years ago, usually seen at weekends with two children in tow, getting them in and out the car to ferry them to whatever activities they did, smiling and laughing just as now only younger. No surprise that someone as clever and kind as a doctor seemed to have her life all worked out.
' People come and go, your house has had a fair few people living in it in the past thirty years. But really the village itself remains pretty unchanged. You have the people whose family have lived here for generations- I don't need to tell you who they are, they will tell you themselves, and incomers like us who live here and commute to jobs elsewhere.' Sandy explained.
'Yes, my husband has transferred his job to Cambridge and I can work from home with mine. Is it just the two of you. Do you have children?'
'Yes, two, girls both in their twenties and living in the towns they went to university at, both teachers. Neither felt like following us into doctoring. And a son, fourteen, quite a late surprise, who is currently at football. I'm sure you will meet him at some point, he is usually seen on his mountain bike riding the bridle paths trying to break the land speed record.' She paused to thank her husband as he brought the drinks in and left silently, ' But don't worry, he is very

considerate of walkers, have to be in a village, everyone knows your parents and aren't afraid to tell them if you misbehave. Us parents would say it is a major advantage of village life, I'm not sure the offspring would agree.'
All too quickly, the pleasant half hour ended and her husband popped his head around the door to say they must be going for their lunch reservation.

Chapter 10

She sat reading Miss Marple. She sat with her back against a tree, so close to the water that if she stuck her foot out, she could reach the water. As always, once she started reading, she was lost in the book and oblivious to what was happening around her, so much so that she didn't notice on the other side of the pond there was someone else sitting, she didn't even notice when he stood up and stripped down to his underwear before climbing into the pond and swimming. In fact she didn't even notice when he climbed out again and returned to his previous spot and pulled a paperback of his own from a pocket and started reading, drying off, still in just his underwear. He however, had noticed her, and his attention was divided between his book and the girl sitting on the opposite side of the pond so intent on her book that she wasn't even aware of his presence.
The irony being that just across the pond from her was the modern byronesque hero she had been dreaming of. There he sat, his slightly too long (for the likes of her Gran and Dad) dark hair in disarray after his swim, his body muscular and honed and his eyes a piercing blue. Had he been a character in a book she read, he would have been the hero, and yet, she didn't even notice his presence.
She read without break in concentration until she finished the book, then glanced at her watch, gasped, hurried to her feet and rushed off. She had only left herself thirteen minutes to do a walk which had taken her fifteen. She hoped she was not late and didn't anger her Dad and Sheryl.
Her walk back, being taken at a far more rapid speed, took her only ten minutes and she was a couple of minutes early. She came in the door and closed it quietly behind her, before she could call out her presence, her dad greeted her with the information Sheryl was

resting and she should prepare them all some lunch and dinner. Entering the kitchen, she looked around seeing mugs and plates with biscuit crumbs on realised clearing up after her dad and Sheryl was also unspoken on her to do list. She looked in the fridge, found some sandwich meat and salad ingredients and quickly put together ham and lettuce sandwiches with cucumber and tomato by the side. She poured three glasses of apple juice and took the plates and glasses through to the dining room where her dad and Sheryl were waiting. The three sat and ate together in silence before her dad disappeared when the telephone rang, and Sheryl announced she needed to rest. Returning to the kitchen, she washed up the lunch dishes and previous washing up then looked in the fridge and freezer for ideas for dinner. The fridge contained very little and the freezer seemed to mainly contain frozen chips, burgers and battered fish. She thought she had better check with someone before she decided and wandered through to her Dad's study. He was sitting at a desk and seemed unimpressed with her ideas for dinner. Sheryl, he felt, deserved a freshly cooked meal. He seemed uninterested in the lack of fresh option to cook and just sighed and said whatever she thought would have to do and that she was welcome to go for a walk or whatever she wanted before dinner. And to make sure she hadn't made a mess for Sheryl to clear up. He then returned his attention to the newspaper in front of him without any further indication of what she should do, so she quietly left the room and decided to return to the quiet pond she found earlier to read for another couple of hours. She did not dare go upstairs to leave the book she had already finished and worried leaving it downstairs might be seen as leaving mess for Sheryl to clear up, so took both books with her again as she left. Retracing her steps from earlier, she walked down the footpath and back to the pond. Looking behind her from her seat earlier, she realised she was visible from the main path. She could see a path weaving its way around the pond and decided to follow it and hopefully find a more hidden spot. She followed the trodden grass around the pond and looked back to where she was sitting earlier, the main footpath was no longer visible. As she walked into the clearing she saw a man, only a few years older than her sitting on a fallen log, staring at her, smiling.
'I'm sorry, should I not be here?' She asked hesitantly, 'I wasn't doing any harm, I just wanted somewhere to read.' Looking up at him, her

heart started to beat faster. It seemed to her over active imagination that Damerel had come to life.
'Me too,' he replied, holding up a dog eared paperback. I come here to read too. And sometimes I come to swim and play my guitar here too.' He smiled at her. 'I don't know you, are you new around here? I'm Jasper.'
"Jasper?' she replied, her heart beating harder, just like Damerel. It was fate.
'Yes, Jasper.' he said. 'You are welcome to join me, I often come here to read.' With that he returned to his book and left her to choose whether she would leave or remain.
Feeling very brave, she sat at the other end of the log and tried to immerse herself in her book. But while her pages might have been the Chalet School, her mind was Georgette Heyer. She kept taking surreptitious glances at him. He was a very attractive man. And the book he was reading was a Terry Prachett. She had read one of them, that was in the school library, she had really enjoyed it. Maybe she could use the book token she got for her birthday last week to buy one. Hopefully, her Dad would take her to Fenland Market and she could find one in a bookshop. She hadn't seen any evidence of books in her dad's house, he had never been a reader and she didn't know if Sheryl was a reader. Her (admittedly) prejudiced opinion would be that she wasn't.
She had forgotten to look back at her book, and he turned and looked at her.
'Would you like to talk?' he asked her. 'I won't disturb you if you would rather read, but you don't seem to be reading.'
Blushes covered her face and she struggled to answer. 'I'm so sorry,' she stammered. 'I didn't mean to be rude. I don't want to disturb you.'
He closed his book, and held out his hand, 'Friends?' he asked.
Blushing even deeper, she took his hand to shake. 'Friends.' She whispered.
And with that her fate was sealed.

Chapter 11

It didn't take long to reach the pub. It was in the next village around a mile away. It sat (as most pubs do) at the cross roads on a corner. The pub looked as though it had had a modern extension trying to keep to the traditional feel but modern building regulations gave it

away. The walls were far thicker and it was set back a brick or two from the rest of the frontage. As her husband parked the car, she commented on how lovely was.
To get from the car park to the pub, they had to walk through a large beer garden where a few families were sitting around picnic benches with drinks while children played on apparatus. She smiled naturally at the happy noises the children were making and quite a few mothers smiled back at her. Her husband, of course, had on his usual public look of good cheer and an arm around her. He nodded at the fathers as he passed them, but steered her towards the inside.
Inside, the clientele were very different, far older. Most of the people sitting down ready to eat inside were middle-aged if not older. Most of the women were wearing far smarter clothing than she was, she noticed. The men were also dressed smarter than her husband, he too was in jeans with a smart polo neck, but many of the men wore shirts, and even ties (although jackets had been removed in deference to the season and weather.
They went to the bar, to order drinks and were soon sitting at their table with their drinks. Although he had driven to the pub, she fully expected to drive back (luckily the route was exceptionally easy and she had no fears of taking a wrong turn). He sat sipping a local bitter (she knew this was another attempt at fitting in as he couldn't stand drinks with fizz in, his preferred drink being a short of any spirit, red wine, or port). She had ordered a lemonade (not sharing his dislike for fizzy drinks) and found it was settling her slightly queasy feeling which she put down to nerves. They looked at the short menu in front of them, as it was a Sunday, the offerings were various roasts, beef, pork, lamb, chicken, salmon or nutroast as the main offering, with stuffing, yorkshire pudding, vegetables and gravy. She decided on chicken, and told her husband, as he preferred to order for both of them and would sometimes change her order if he didn't think it was suitable.
Soon they were eating a huge meal that she knew she could not finish, there sadly hadn't been a smaller plate option. Luckily, her husband was happy to eat most of her meat, along with the two glasses of red wine he ordered himself through the meal, leaving her a more manageable amount. He still frowned in annoyance that her plate held food when she had finished. But looking around at the plates being cleared, she could see she was not the only person to be

unable to finish the huge portions. Frowning at her in annoyance, he ordered himself another drink, a double whisky this time.
Hearing this, her mood fell. For some reason, whisky seemed to bring out the worst in her husband. Hopefully, he would sleep it off this afternoon, otherwise, she knew she was in for a bad afternoon.
After he had finished his drink, they headed back to the car. As she drove home, he started yawning. This was her opportunity.
'Why don't you go home and have a rest, you've worked so hard at this move. I will pop into town and get us some shopping before the shops close, early closing on a Sunday. '
To her relief, he agreed with her suggestion and once home, stretched out on the sofa with the newspaper and TV remote, while she got her things together and went out to the small Ford Ka parked beside her husband's larger more executive car. She had had the car since it was new, a guilty present from her father when she passed her driving test. One of the last presents she had from him before he went to work abroad and gradually lost touch with her. She didn't drive much in London, her Gran's, work and the local high street had all been within a few minute's walk or a couple of tube stops. She had hoped the Ka signified the start of a better, closer relationship between her father and her, but that hadn't happened. She opened the car and set off in the opposite direction to the pub for the town, where there would surely be a supermarket open.
After shopping and filling the small boot of the Ka with a mixture of necessities and meal ingredients, she picked up two bottles of vitamins and headed for the bin. She emptied the first bottle of vitamins into the bin, filled the bottle with the vitamins from the first and threw away the second bottle. She took out a separate receipt with just one item on and threw that in the bin too. The then put the bottle back in the boot of her car with the rest of the shopping and sat in the driver's seat. She pulled out a mobile phone and dialled a number.
'Claire? It is me. Yes, we arrived last night but I couldn't call then.' She paused while the other person was speaking, 'I know. I'm sorry. This is the first chance I've had to call. ' again she listened. 'He has been really kind, just like he used to be when we first met him. Maybe this is just what we need.' listening and nodding her head. '*She* is still in London, so at least I know *that* can't be an issue any more.' Fast blinking as she listened. 'I know, it is lonely up here, but

lots of couples make a new life in new places and he said we could talk about having a baby.' Listening again. 'Thank you, I miss you too. I will find a way to meet up, I promise. Thank you. I will call in the week.'
It would be much easier to call in the week when he was at work, and as Claire also worked for the same company it would be a call to her work number, although she still hadn't tackled him not wanting her to work. She had to carry on working. For one thing, his salary alone would not sustain the lifestyle he liked to live. Although she knew better than to criticise him in that way.
And they needed to have that chat about babies, soon.
She drove home, psyching herself up to be brave later when he had slept off the effects of a big meal and the effects of whisky.

Chapter 12
' The Chalet school in Exile? Never heard of that? ' He asked questioningly.
She blushed bright red, so embarrassed, why hadn't she read that this morning? Now she looked like a little kid reading a little kid book. He would never want to know her after that.
'It is about people escaping the Nazi's, English people living in Austria and building a new life.' She said leaving out the entire Chalet School part which made it sound so much less childish.
'I'd like to escape here, ' he said. ' This place may as well be run by the Nazis. A load of old women who spy on you and tell your Mum everything you do that they don't approve of- and they approve of nothing. That is why I come here, no one knows about it and they would never hike through the brambles like we did to get here. And it is far enough from the main path, they can't hear you either.'
She felt concerned briefly that people might have seen them despite his assurance that no one could see or hear them here. What if someone told her Dad? Then she realised, her dad probably wouldn't care anyway, it kept her out of his way. Then she felt great, she and Jasper had a secret place no one knew about, their own secret and they were friends. 'Terry Prachett?' she asked, 'I've read one of his, it was really good, but it was the only one in the school library. I got a book token early for my birthday, I was thinking of buying a Terry Prachett book with that. Maybe I will see if Dad will take me into Fenland Market to buy one.'

He laughed.
She felt horrified, was it that transparent that she only wanted to read Terry Prachett because he was?
'No bookshop there.' he said. 'But there are a few charity shops where you can pick up second hand books cheaply.'
'No bookshop?'She looked horrified again.'Not one?'
'Nope.' he smiled, raising his eyebrows, 'No bookshop. No nightclub, no cinema, no bowling, no fun!'
She had a feeling her dad hadn't brought her here to have fun, and even if there was all of that, she didn't think there would be many fun trips there. She felt pretty sure her most exciting times might be now, sitting by the pond with one of the best looking men she had ever met and discussing books. 'It is a really small town then?' She asked.
'Yep. Not really worth the bother. A few historical buildings, a market and a few shops and old fashioned pubs and restaurants. Some of the historical buildings are interesting though. But mainly it was ruined by modernisation. Anyway, Fenland Market and here are boring. I haven't seen you before today, so who are you, and how come you ended up here?'
Usually she was shy and quiet, she found herself opening up to him and telling him all about her family and why she was here. She had never found anyone so easy to talk to.
'I know how hard it is to lose a parent, my dad is gone.' He said looking intently at her (leaving out that gone didn't mean dead like her mum but had left).
Her heart swelled, he understood how she felt. None of her friends had that experience, she had felt so alone. People were kind, but they expected her to be over it by now, it was a couple of years ago, they didn't really understand apart from Gran who missed her just as much and who she knew sobbed quietly at night when she was in bed. And now Jasper.
No afternoon had ever gone by as fast, they talked and laughed, she felt as though she had known him forever. Not only did he understand, but he was a keen reader too. They had read lots of the same books, he liked Agatha Christie too, he had read Swallows and Amazons as a child, and the Hardy Boys to her Nancy Drew. He loved horror stories, James Herbert was another author they had both read. They both loved The Magic Cottage.

She truly felt she had met her modern day Damerel. She wondered if he had read Venetia? He seemed to have read so much that she had, and other more modern things that weren't really on the shelves at home and she didn't know if they were in the library at school. She knew her school library was conservative in taste, they didn't even have the Sweet Valley High books she and her friends had read constantly when they were younger (and she still reread as a comfort read, like her Chalet School and Nancy Drew books). One of her friends had asked the librarian if they could get the 'Flowers in the Attic' series in the library, but after looking into it, the school had decided it wasn't suitable. Lots of her friends had read them and really enjoyed them, they had got them from the local library or bought them. The first one didn't ever seem to be in the library and she had planned to spend her book token from her birthday on that until Jasper and his Terry Prachett book today had changed her mind. Maybe she would have enough to buy both and maybe she could spend some of her birthday money on second hand books in the charity shops, they might have Terry Prachett, James Herbert or some of the other authors Jasper had mentioned.

Chapter 13

When she reached home, he was asleep on the sofa, his phone face down beside him. She resisted the urge to look at it despite it repeatedly vibrating.

She thought back to that day, only three months ago that her life had shattered.

She was home from work as usual just before six. Before she started dinner, she decided to check her e mails, she was waiting for an e mail from a distant cousin on her dad's side who had a newborn. She had texted earlier to say she had e mailed some photos through- and a couple of old photos with her Mum and Dad in. It was the only contact she had with her Dad's family. She was looking forward to seeing the baby photos but also to see the photos of her mum not much younger than she was now.

She had switched on the shared computer in the living room, but her husband had not logged his e mail out, his in box came up and the top message subject was 'sexxxy pics from the weekend babe x' . Her heart was racing as she opened the message. She recognised the woman in the photos immediately. It was one of his work colleagues. The one who he had to work late with a lot- tonight included. She looked through the photos, it wasn't just Nikki, but her husband as well, dressed up in the suit she had taken to be dry cleaned earlier, kissing Nikki with his hand inside her half undone shirt. She didn't know how long she had sat there looking at these photos, tears cascading silently down her face.

She didn't hear the front door open or see her husband come into the room. The first time she was aware of him was when he roughly grabbed her from the computer chair and turned her to face him. He was shouting and shaking her, she felt detached from it, as though she was watching it from outside. She felt herself pushed onto the sofa, he was still shouting at her and holding her down. She tried to sit up but he wouldn't let her. She realised that his hand on her arm was hurting her, and tried to tell him, he slapped her around the face. He had never hit her, or hurt her physically before. She really must have done something terrible.

Then she heard a ripping sound and felt his hand pressing down on her neck. By providence, she didn't remember what happened next, just feeling so sore down there and him zipping up his trousers. When she stood up, she felt wet between her legs and saw a mixture of semen and blood running down her legs and it hurt. In a trance she went and cleaned herself up and dressed. She would go to Gran's, Gran would help her and explain what happened. James had never behaved like that before, he had always been so kind. Gran would be able to help her. She really must have done something terrible to make him hurt her there, like that.

She walked back downstairs and the phone was ringing. Automatically, she picked it up, she noticed James was at the computer.

'Mrs Granger?' A formal voice said, 'Next of kin for Mrs Masterton?'

'Yes.' she said mechanically, aware that whatever came next would not be good.

'I'm very sorry to inform you, your Grandma has been brought to North Middlesex Hospital, a suspected stroke...'

She had no idea what else was said she literally dropped the phone, picked up her car keys and left the house without saying another word. She just knew she had to be with Gran. And with Gran she had stayed until a second stroke a month ago had claimed her.

She had never spoken with him about what she had seen, he had spoken of it, told her it was a mistake, it was over and that he had already put their house on the market, he would be getting a transfer and they would be moving away to make a new start. Have the family she wanted and apparently now he did too. She couldn't really take in what he was saying, her mind had been taken up with Gran. She mechanically signed the papers he had given her and now she had found herself here. Gran had always said marriage is hard and you have to work at it. Gran said marriage is forever. Gran hadn't approved of divorce, she thought people should work at their problems. She had never spoken of infidelity or physical abuse, or the other thing that had happened. But all of that seemed unimportant compared to the loss of Gran, the one person left who had truly loved her.
She realised she was still watching her husband sleeping and moved into the kitchen area to unpack the shopping and start on an evening meal. Even though they had eaten a large lunch, she knew her husband would expect a meal prepared for dinner.
As she prepared the salad and potatoes for dinner her husband woke up. He looked over to her and then picked up his phone.
'I'd love a cup of coffee while you are there, love.' he said.
'Of course.' she replied and hurried to provide him with one before returning to the food. 'What time would you like dinner? She asked, it is all prepared, I just need to steam the fish and potatoes.'
'Later, ' he said irritably, ' eight or so, I won't be hungry until then after our excellent lunch.'
'That is fine. Could we talk about what you said yesterday?' she said sitting down next to him on the sofa, 'about starting a family.'
He rolled his eyes, 'Baby mad!' I think you are more in love with the idea of having a baby than with me!'
'No, no, but you said yesterday. And we always said we would have children after we had been married a couple of years, and it had been almost ten years now. I'm thirty.' She said trying not to cry.
'And I'm forty and I'm not in a rush, why are you? What is it with women and reaching thirty that you all think it is time to pop some babies out? I see it all the time at work, perfectly good girl, pretty with a nice figure pops out the babies and all she can think of is the blasted kids and goes to seed.'
I won't let myself go, I will be careful about my weight. '

'I've heard that before! And anyway, I've noticed recently that stomach isn't looking as flat as before. Not even a baby as an excuse! And don't you go thinking about poking holes in that diaphragm, I've heard of women doing that.'
'I wouldn't.' she said fighting back tears.
'Don't cry. Love. Can't you take a little joke! Nothing to cry about, we will have a baby soon. It just isn't fair of you to push and manipulate me with those tears. Be a good girl and go clean up, can't have a neighbour popping round and seeing you not looking your best.'

Chapter 14

The afternoon continued, the summer idyll she had imagined. A friend who she could laugh with and talk about books. So many authors they had both read.
He had even read Dennis Wheatley and liked the Duc as much as she did! Then they got onto Sherlock Holmes, and The Hound of the Baskervilles. They had both watched the same television adaption with Jeremy Brett too.
Never had she had a friend who she could talk about so many books with, a friend who understood her so well. He was 18, he was looking for a job. He had done A levels but wasn't going to university, he wanted to earn money and get away from the village, there was nothing here for him. He had an evening shift at a petrol station and he was saving as much as he could after giving his ma some money for his keep. She didn't have much money, he explained. They lived in the row of council houses at the end of the village, most of them had been bought, but not theirs and not his nan's, they were still council houses. His nan was retired, she had worked the land, and his ma cycled each weekday to the local sugar beet factory. She had him too young and had had to work hard. He didn't want a life like hers. He'd been made fun of at school, no dad, no money, no car, no school trips, no clubs, no scouts, second hand clothes and no ma home when he finished school. He had always been in trouble at school, fighting back when they said things. It was always his fault. Their mums could come in, their dads write letters with authority. His ma hadn't finished school, she wasn't confident to stand up for him to the teachers- some of them had been her teachers. His nan wouldn't get involved either she didn't think much

of education or teachers, so he had to fend for himself. He didn't really have friends at school, their parents didn't approve of him, he wasn't the right sort, so he had read a lot, borrowing books from the library, mowing lawns and cleaning cars from the time he was ten to try to earn some pocket money (ma didn't earn enough to have any left for that) and often give mum some too to help with the bills or shopping. He'd bought himself a second hand bike and bike lock that he used to get to work, and if you couldn't walk or cycle it, he didn't go.
She felt so sorry for him, she had lost a parent too, and her other was uninterested, but Gran was always there. They weren't rich in her eyes- compared to her friends, but there was a large comfy house which was always kept warm, cinema trips in the holidays, new uniform when she outgrew it, friends and lots of kindness from teachers and friends, and offers of lifts even though gran had a car, and teachers telling her privately that if a trip was too expensive to let them know and they were sure there was help. No educational trip had ever been too expensive, even the day trip to France. She realised now how lucky she was. She knew it wasn't just her. When Lisa's dad had lost his job, she knew the school had helped her to go on trips and even bought her younger sister a new blazer at the start of high school as she was the same size as Lisa and there was no blazer to hand down yet. She had taken all these things for granted. She hadn't realised not every school was as kind to every child. And Father Dominic had spoken to Gran too, said to let him know if there was anything they couldn't afford. Although thinking about it, Dad had a good job, had bought a large house, surely he was paying for these things? Shouldn't he be? Maybe she should ask Gran when she got back to London. She suddenly felt guilty for everything she had taken for granted and worried Gran was struggling because of her. Then a memory from a history lesson flashed into her mind. The Victorians had judged the poor. Some were the deserving poor and they were given assistance, while the ones viewed as the undeserving poor were not. She wondered why his neighbours had viewed them as the undeserving poor while her and her Gran (who weren't really poor when you thought about it, Gran owned her house and there was always enough money for necessities and a little fun) were viewed by their community as deserving. It seemed strange that any family could be viewed as undeserving anyway,

especially with the dad gone and the mum working hard to make ends meet. Apart from Jasper, she didn't feel she would like this village or the people who lived here much.
Very soon, instead of sitting on opposite ends of the log, the were sitting together in the middle, reading his Terry Prachett book together. She was more determined than ever to buy one with her book token.
All too soon, the afternoon had gone and she realised she should be going back to cook dinner. And he needed to head to work for his shift. They started planning for meeting the following day, he said the weather forecast was hot so he planned to swim, he suggested she brought her swim things with her too. They agreed to meet at eleven the following morning- he slept late after his shift.
She walked home excited, she had never swum anywhere but in the local pool they had swimming lessons with school and a couple of times at the beach. The idea of swimming in a pond seemed very exciting. She was glad she had packed her swimming costumes. Her way home was spent trying to decide which of them she should bring the next day. Of course she wanted to look nice for him. For once, her head was filled with the present and a real person rather than book born fantasies.
In all too short a time she was home and 'helping' prepare dinner which was to be a spaghetti bolognese (she was very grateful for the jar of sauce and its useful instructions as she had no idea other than mince, tomato and onion you put in to make one- her helping at home usually being fetching and preparing ingredients rather than making the dish, she was grateful for her cookery lessons at school - where they had once made one- and the jar's instructions, otherwise she might not have known to fry the onion and mince prior to adding the sauce).
Her dad complimented Sheryl highly on the meal- she remembered it had always been a favourite meal of his, but when her mum (or gran) made it, there was no sauce jar. She felt a little aggrieved that Sheryl took all the compliments when at the first sight of the mince, she had excused herself from the room, claiming nausea, and had not returned until the smell of the simmering dish had permeated the house. She felt even more irritated when her dad told her she should learn from Sheryl's wonderful cooking as she didn't want to just be cooking old fashioned meals like her gran when she got married.

After dinner, and clearing up, she was again sent to her bedroom and read her rationed chapter of Venetia (knowing Gran would be reading it too) and mulled on her own summer idyll. She wished she could tell Gran about Jasper, but the sensible side of her also knew Gran would be concerned by a secret friendship in a secret place between her and an eighteen year old man. She wondered if she would be allowed to ring Gran (after six of course) one evening. Just to let her know she was ok and to check Gran was ok. Maybe she would ask at dinner tomorrow, she didn't think going back downstairs would to ask would be taken well. She had brought a pad of paper with her, maybe she could write Gran a letter as well, although without mentioning Jasper (or exactly how helpful she was being expected to be) there wasn't very much she could write. Maybe a phone call would be best. And Gran never chattered on the phone, she was from a generation where phone calls were three minutes only and she had never managed to understand the chatting the younger generation did on the phone.
Settling down with Mr Standfast by John Buchan, she lay on the covers and read, maybe she would ask if she could read in the garden tomorrow night too, she wouldn't disturb anyone that way and it felt very early to be in bed at 8.30pm especially when it was so light outside.

Chapter 15

Cleaned up, and meeting her husband's approval, dinner prepared and his coffee cup in the dishwasher, she acceded to his demand for them to take a walk, there were a network of paths connecting different ends of the village and the next village.
Wearing trainers on her feet (which earned her a frown from her husband but unless the paths had improved greatly, she didn't think she would be able to safely walk them in heels), they set off. She was very aware, he had no actual desire to go for a walk, let alone go for a walk with her, but that he felt that is what people would be doing early evening on a Sunday and he wanted to meet people and project the right image. Projecting the right image had always been an obsession of his. She hadn't realised it until after they were engaged when he started to check her clothing choices before they went out. As he explained to her, her choices reflected on him. He

liked to convey a certain image, and now she too was part of that. Soon that became checking her friends were suitable and that jobs she was applying for were suitable too. At the time, applying for jobs for the first time straight out of university and newly married, she had been grateful that her husband took such care of her. In the last few years, she had questioned his guidance which seemed to be more about ensuring she was with people he viewed as suitable than actually beneficial to her career path. And while many of the people he viewed as unsuitable (not that I'd ever try to control who your friends are but surely you must see that we could never invite someone like that to a meal with my work colleagues, what would they think?) had over time disappeared, her closest friend, Claire, had gone nowhere.
She had known Claire since early childhood. Claire's mum and her mum had been friends from school. They had married and had children at around the same time. Claire and her were in the same class at primary school and although they were in different forms at secondary school, they were in top sets together and took the same GCSE's and A levels and then went onto university to do the same course, both staying living at home and commuting together each day. While they had chosen different companies to start their career in (with careful guidance from her husband), they had for the past six years both worked together at the same company, in the same department. That had been the second secret she had kept from her husband. Somehow, she had felt it wiser not to mention that they now worked together. Without her suggesting it, neither her gran, Claire or Claire's family had ever mentioned it to him either.
Claire wasn't someone people generally disapproved of. Her hair was its natural blonde, she had had no surgical enhancements. Her make up was minimal and she had no tattoos. She was polite, intelligent, quietly spoken, from a 'good catholic family' (she was the eldest of six, the youngest currently being in his final year of university) whose father was in the army and mother worked part time as a teacher. She had had a boyfriend who was in the army when James had first met her, he was also older- about the same age as James and they had married the year after she had married James. But from the day James had met her, it had been clear to everyone that James did not like Claire. Of course, he always denied it, but it had been as clear as day.

He had sighed when Claire was her one bridesmaid. Sighed again when she was Claire's Maid of Honour. And again when she was godmother to Claire's oldest child (she was sure he would sigh again in a few months when she became godmother to Claire's second child). Without saying a word against her, he managed to make meeting up awkward with emergencies or work events he had not previously mentioned. Luckily, Claire was as comfortable at Gran's as she was at her own home and as well as lunch together at work, they tended to bump into each other at Gran's and church. So after ten years of her marriage they were as close as ever.
Claire generally said nothing about James unless it was nice. But that had all changed three months previously when Claire joined her at the hospital to sit with her and Gran following the stroke. Claire's eyes had taken in the bruises around her neck, the bruises on her face, the bruises on her arms. That night, at Gran's, Claire had walked into the bathroom where Claire was bathing, trying to soothe her bleeding while sobbing for her Gran. Claire had walked in and seen the blood, the bruising, and the scratches. Claire had been plain in her opinion and her opinion was not that of the Catholic Church they had grown up in. Divorce was not a bad word in Claire's eyes when your husband had behaved that way.
Claire had told her husband and family. She had known they knew at Gran's funeral when they held her as lovingly as ever but were cold to James. When they reassured her she wasn't alone, when they told her they were her family. And when James had laughingly said that surely he was her family, Claire's second brother had turned and left the room, his face red with fury. But despite their assurances, she knew that really she was alone. Or would be alone if she walked away from James. No real family and the disapproval of God.
She walked with James down the paths she had trodden all those years ago. The horses were still in the field where they had been, she idly wondered if they were the same horses, she had no idea how long horses lived but there was one brown and one white just as there had been then. Two women, about her age, were in the field with the horses, they raised their hand in greeting as they passed. They followed the footpath and she spied the wooded area which had held the pond. It was too overgrown now to see the pond at all from the path, so she was spared a view of *that*. A man walked towards them as they walked down the path, for a moment her heart

pounded, she wouldn't have to face Jasper? As he came closer, she saw he was too young, younger than her, and nothing like him. It was fear, a trick of the light, that had made her panic briefly.
Her husband reached out and took her hand, they walked together with him commenting on their surroundings (mainly the state of the path rather than the wildlife) and how wise she had been to wear trainers (which made her smile wryly inside).
She realised now, she would always have another secret from her husband, she could not tell him that this had been the village she had stayed with her father. The time to tell him had gone. And it was too intimately connected with the first secret. The secret only Gran and the Priest had known. Did all women have secrets from their husbands? Was it her keeping secrets that had poisoned their marriage? Is that why he had done all those things? Was it her fault? She realised he was speaking to her and turned her full attention to him. He did not like it when her mind was elsewhere. They walked on together, him planning a house-warming to meet the neighbours and her putting together the finer details.

Chapter 16

She woke early, long before her dad or Sheryl was awake, she crept downstairs, emptied the dishwasher and set up the cups for coffee along with the percolator. Then she quietly opened the back door and stepped outside into the quiet morning. She sat on a plastic patio chair listening to the dawn chorus. She watched the collared doves and wood pigeons perching on the nearby roofs and fences. She smiled at the antics of the smaller birds vying for space on their neighbour's bird table. The world seemed peaceful and beautiful. Soon, her neighbour's children came outside and started playing. She had seen them coming and going, the oldest was only a few years younger than her, a couple of years ago they might have been friends, playing and chatting together but they seemed very young playing childish games still.
Hearing movement inside, she stepped inside to see her Dad in his work suit coming into the kitchen. He put on the percolator and made himself a cup of coffee.
'Keep quiet will you, Sheryl would like a lie-in. And give her a hand

with dinner. I think she is going out with some friends for lunch so you'll have to sort yourself out, there are things to make sandwiches around. I suppose you will meet up and play with other village kids your age. Sheryl suggested you might want to leave your gran's and come to school up here to help out with your baby brother, but it turns out it isn't that easy on the GCSE courses and your headteacher was most rude about the suggestion.'

Move up there? Her heart sank. Even for Damer- Jasper- she didn't want to leave her Gran and her friends to move here. She knew very well she wouldn't be having fun, she'd be doing her school work and then the housework and childcare as Sheryl would be too tired or busy. 'I think finishing my GCSEs in London is best, Dad. My school is one of the best for getting girls into good universities, and I would like to go to university and get a degree. I haven't decided what yet, English Literature maybe, or something to do with history or religion.'

'I'd have thought you'd be more concerned with helping with your little brother than all that nonsense. ' He seemed annoyed as he left his half-finished coffee on the side and started walking to the door.

'Dad, could I call Gran tonight? I really miss her.' She suddenly felt her throat was too full. What if he said no?

'If you must.' he scowled. 'Most girls your age would be glad to have a bit of freedom.' He left the house, slamming the door behind him, despite Sheryl's lie-in.

She quietly went upstairs and dressed, packing her swimming things (she took both costumes and a towel) and *Mr Standfast*. Back downstairs, it was still only 8am, so she took her book and sat outside.

As soon as she heard noise upstairs, she returned inside and made Sheryl a cup of coffee which she took upstairs. Sheryl, to her surprise, was up and choosing clothes. She took the coffee with a brief thank you and returned to choosing her clothes.

Downstairs, a few minutes later, Sheryl left the coffee cup on the side and frowned at her. 'I'm going out with my friends today. You can have the spare key so you can come and go. There is bolognese left from last night so we can have that for dinner tonight. Make yourself a sandwich or something for lunch.' And Sheryl too left the house.

It was still only 9am. She suddenly remembered seeing a phone box

at the other end of the village. She had put her swimming kit in her bag which also held her purse. She decided to walk down to the phone box and call Gran. Four minutes later she was dialling the familiar number- having remembered to start with the area code.
'Gran, it is me.... yes, I'm fine, are you?... In a phonebox. In the village... I miss you...I love you too... yes fine, they are very busy... ok I suppose... not unkind. Sheryl is pregnant... yes they want a boy... I want to come home too... I love you, bye..'
Her two ten pence pieces didn't seem to last very long. She wished she was back in London with Gran. But she wished she could take Jasper with her. After the call, she realised she hadn't even mentioned Jasper. She had never hidden anything from Gran before.
She didn't see the point in going back to the house, so she decided to explore the footpaths around the village for a couple of hours. Other than a few dog walkers the paths seemed empty, and she soon discovered she had no need to walk through the village to reach the footpath, another footpath marked on a map took her to a few metres from the house.
She checked the footpath and where she was going then decided she may as well sit and read by the pond, after all, she had Mr Standfast with her.
When she reached the pond, she was surprised to find she was not the only one enjoying the early morning delights of the day. A family of ducks was swimming across the pond- mallards, Mother, Father and six ducklings. She was enchanted by the babies and put her book aside to quietly watch their antics. Another family of ducks came and joined them providing more entertainment.
When they swam out of sight she returned to her book but read it superficially, hoping Jasper would arrive soon.

Chapter 17

Back at the house after their walk, she realised she needed to write down his plans and guest list if this party was to occur. The list was mainly couples,his friends, from his work. She added Claire and family to the list and he frowned.
'There won't be space for them to stay, and it is too far to drive from London.' He announced. 'three spare rooms and I've filled them all already.'
Usually, she would let this go and accede to his demands, but her

friendship with Claire was something she thought was worth fighting for. 'Then you will need to cut one of the couples from your list. If this is *our* house-warming, I too have a choice on the guest list.'
His eyes narrowed. 'I've already invited them, so it is too late.'
'Then choose who you want to uninvite or you can organise this party yourself without any help from me and without my presence.' Her heart was pounding in her chest, she had never stood against him like that.
He looked her up and down with derision. His hand reached out and held her wrist hard, twisting it slightly. He spoke slowly and quietly but with a hint of menace. 'I don't think you really want to do that. After all, you have no job here, no friends here. So we ***will*** be having the party and we will be having the people I have invited. And you will be organising it and smiling through it. Is that clear?'
Tears pricked in her eyes as she remembered the last time she had angered him. 'Is. That. Clear?' He repeated slowly as you might to a disobedient child. His grip on her wrist tightened further- she had no doubt he meant her to notice.
She turned her eyes down to the pad of paper, he let go of her wrist and took the paper and pen from her. He firmly crossed out 'Claire and family' then returned the pad to her.
'We will have it next weekend, you have the week to prepare it, *you* might need to say you can't do this ridiculous work from home job, our priority should be *my* career, especially if you want a child eventually.' Her hands unconsciously stroked her flat stomach when she said that and her face relaxed slightly. Another secret. 'We will have a barbecue. Steak, chops, sausages, burgers, salmon, and you can spend a few minutes on those salads you women like- potato salad, pasta salad and a couple of others. A fruit salad, cheesecake and pavlova for dessert, shouldn't take you long. Breads with the meats too, crisps, dips and other bits. Obviously, you need to finish unpacking and make the house look a bit more characterful. Did you say you'd organised furniture?.' She nodded. 'That should keep you busy this week. Anyway, I think I will have a bath while you sort out the dinner.' He kissed her on the forehead and walked out of the room.
She looked at her wrist. It was red from where he had held it and she was very aware it would bruise. Tears pricked in her eyes and overran. She sat with tears rolling down her face hearing the bath

upstairs running. Then his phone vibrated, he had left it on the table. She turned it over and saw the message pop up. 'Can't wait to see you tomorrow, all of you! Nikki xxx.' Quickly, she picked up her phone and photographed the message. She turned his phone back over without opening it up. Tears continued rolling down her face. She could hear him in the bath and took the opportunity to message Claire. She knew now that Claire was right, whatever her religion told her, it was time to escape this marriage. But, for the first time in her life, she wasn't prepared to go quietly and without making a fuss. For fifteen minutes, they messaged back and forth, then she went back over her messages and deleted every one of them. Tomorrow, when he was at work, they would talk some more, but in the meantime, she had a plan.

While she prepared the dinner, she thought back to when they had first been together. They had met him through an acquaintance- Jenny- at university. They had all gone to Jenny's engagement party in a posh banqueting hall in West London, James was a friend of a cousin of Jenny's and had been invited along too. Claire, Jenny (who was a mature student) and her were on the same course. James came to ask her to dance and spent the rest of the evening with her. He asked for her number and rang her the next day, he was so handsome and witty. He seemed much more mature than the boys her age who she went to university with and he was a Catholic too so never tried to pressure her, he thought waiting for marriage was the right thing to do. Little did she know that only applied to her, not him.

He visited her at Gran's, picked her up and took her out. He introduced both her and Gran to his (now deceased) parents. Gran liked his parents very much, but never really voiced an opinion on James. She had presumed Gran liked him, but the letter that had been alongside the will had suggested a different story. Gran had particularly liked the pre nuptial contract, urging her to sign it (she had been surprised by this considering Gran's anti-divorce stance- surely no one should enter marriage preparing just in case for divorce?) and approving of the clauses to do with inheritance and assets before marriage being protected. At the time she had presumed Gran liked him so much she saw no possibility of divorce and wanted him to know his younger bride was not after his property. Now, she knew better. The money her mother had left and her inheritance from Gran far outweighed the ten thousand pound

equity he had in his property before marriage and his expectations of inheriting (which hadn't come to be) his grandparents property(as the only male heir). Their will had named all grandchildren equally for very little, the majority going to their three children and his parents' part being swallowed in care home fees for his mother's dementia. Her assets and inheritance turned out to be worth far more- a fact her husband was not yet aware of- and clever Gran had safeguarded it all. Not only that, looking back, she realised how blind and deaf she had been to Gran's warnings that maybe James was not the hero she thought him to be.
She had dinner served and on the table by the time he came down and she was prepared to play the part he expected, the loving and subservient wife for a few days even if inside she was filled with sadness and anger at his continuing betrayal.

Chapter 18

It wasn't until a few minutes after eleven that Jasper arrived. By this time she had convinced herself that he wasn't coming. But, of course, he did. He came by bike, she heard the squeak of brakes as he stopped by the entrance to the woodland and the rustle of leaves as he pushed his way through the woodland, carrying his bike on his shoulder. On one handlebar he had a plastic bag which she presumed contained his swimwear and a towel.
He sat down beside her on the log. 'I woke up late.'He said, 'Good job we are going swimming this morning, no time for a shower before I came.'
She didn't really know how to reply to that, she was already aware from his proximity and the gamey smell from him that he hadn't had time for morning ablutions (other than teeth cleaning, there was a blob of toothpaste that had fallen onto his t shirt. 'Shall we swim now?'She asked, deciding it was easier to not respond to the showering comments. 'Did you work very late last night?'
He smiled at her, 'Got home about two, had something to eat and it was about four before I fell asleep, I was reading a bike book.'
'A bike book?'
'My chain is loose, I need to take a link out, it keeps slipping. No Daddy to do it for me.' He spoke bitterly.
'My 'Daddy' has never mended my bike, my mum used to. Now Gran makes me take it to the shop. But we can't really do much riding in

London, just around the park with Claire sometimes on a Saturday morning. Too much traffic. '
'But when you lived with your dad, didn't he do bike stuff with you then?'
'No, he was too busy. But, - I haven't told anyone else this- I found Mum's diaries and I've been reading them. And I think his 'busy' had female names. There are quite a few she mentions. I don't think she was very happy really.'
He reached across and held her arm for a minute in sympathy. 'If I ever marry and have kids, I'm going to make sure I teach my kids- sons to do stuff like mend their bikes, chopping wood, mowing lawns, electrical and plumbing stuff. It all costs so much if you don't have much money to start with. '
'You can teach girls too- my mum did most of that, and gran does too. Grandad died when Mum was a baby and Gran had to do it all- or pay and I don't think she had that much money- so she learnt and taught my mum too. I can do some simple electric and plumbing stuff and Gran taught me to change a tyre on a car. She never rode a bike so she can't help me with bike stuff and she worries I haven't done it right so we take it to the bike shop. But girls need to learn too. Especially if their husband dies like Grandpa or is too *busy* like my dad.'
'Yeah, you are right. Ma has tried to learn but I read books to learn- she isn't so hot at reading- and I try to do stuff for her and Nan. Anyway, it is boiling already, shall we go swimming?'
She nodded then realised a pond didn't come with male and female changing rooms. Before she could voice her concern, he stripped down to a pair of fitting boxer shorts and started wading into the pond.
She looked around, picked a large tree and darted behind it, ignoring the nettles, to change into her swimming clothes and the swimming shoes gran had bought her when they stayed at a pebbly beach last summer. She carefully walked into the water, wondering what the depth would be. She was a good swimmer but in pools. Other than the sea, she hadn't swum apart from in a pool with clear depth markings. The pond seemed to get deeper quite quickly, then stay at about waist or chest depth. There was a slight current from the stream feeding and exiting the pond but nothing difficult to swim against. The bottom seemed to be sandy and pebbly so she didn't

need to worry about being caught in plants and the water was very clear but cold.
They swam around for some time, splashing each other and generally laughing at the smallest of things. The two families of ducks kept a distance and so did the fish Jasper assured her lived within the pond and stream- trout- he had poached a few brown trout in the past. There was a heron sitting on the far side of the pond but he flew off in disgust as they moved closer to him.
After a couple of hours laughing and playing in the water, they were ready to get out. He took her hand to help her out of the pond but didn't let go when they were out. One-handed he pulled a blanket our of his bag and threw it on the ground for them to sit. When they sat he let go of her hand and instead stroked her cheek with one hand before leaning forward and placing a gentle kiss on her lips.
His lips felt soft and gentle. She was too surprised to respond. Jasper was kissing *her!* She looked down shyly as he stopped. He placed his hand under her chin and lifted he face. 'Would you like me to stop?' He asked gently.
She looked in his eyes, feeling her blush rising, her heart hammering in her chest. She shook her head indicating no. Again he gently reached across and kissed her. This time she kissed him back. He extended the kiss, opening his mouth slightly, and she responded. Soon they were kissing passionately with their arms around each other as they dried in the warmth of the day. Lunch was forgotten about as she spent the afternoon holding and kissing him. Barely a word was spoken. It was late afternoon when he disengaged his lips from hers.
'I have to go,' He sighed.'Work is a bit earlier tonight. Can we meet again tomorrow, gorgeous?'
She nodded.
'10am? Wait until I've been gone a few minutes before you leave. We don't want any nosy neighbours to report back to your dad.' He stood, put his hand out and pulled her to her feet. Putting his arm around her, he kissed her deeply again 'I'll be thinking of you tonight. All night.' he winked.
'Me too.' She said shyly.
'And that is just what every man wants.' he leaned in for another kiss. Then picked up his blanket, stuffed it in the carrier bag, stepped into his shorts, pulled his t shirt over his head picked up his bike and

headed off. 'Parting is such sweet sorrow!' He called to her quietly as he walked away.
She took the time to go back behind the tree where her bag of clothes still were and change into her proper clothes before walking home. Upon reaching home, she took the time to have a shower and change into clean clothes before either her dad or Sheryl arrived home and put on a wash, all the clothes she had worn so far, including her swimming things. She had everything washed, dried on the line and put away before Sheryl made it home just after six, about half an hour before her dad was due.

Chapter 19

The next morning, when he had left early for work, she put her plan into action. She took out the décor from their old house and placed it where she knew he would approve. Certain pieces, pieces which had familial significance to her, she packed away in shopping bags and placed in the boot of her car. She then headed upstairs to her bedroom and a couple of bags of clothes,- mainly casual items was also deposited in the boot of her car. She moved the remaining clothes around to hide the gaps.
A few minutes before nine, she headed into Fenland Market, her first stop was a car park used mainly by students. She pulled up beside a nondescript silver hatchback and placed the bags in the boot of the car. She then stopped and chatted for a few minutes to the driver of the car and shared a hug. The silver hatchback then drove off and she headed into town, back to the furniture shops she had previously called.
The gentleman running the shop was hugely helpful and agreed to add the larger items she purchased to her order for delivery that afternoon. A quick stop for some sandwiches and she was ready to head home.
Once home, she wasted no time but was straight on the computer, working. In fact she didn't pause for a break until 3pm and the delivery of the furniture and additional items she had ordered. By five the furniture was in place in the house, fully built and the packaging heading off on the lorry. A few tweaks to the placement of objects and a few minutes with picture hooks and a hammer and she felt the house would please him.
She quickly put in a steamer some new potatoes and made up a bowl of mixed salad. The chicken she could put in the oven, and turn on

the steamer when he came home. He would always want a shower before they sat down to dinner, only now, she realised, it was less about separating work and home and more about making sure his wife didn't discover the perfumed smell of his infidelity. She wondered why he had been so keen to marry her, when clearly his wedding vows meant so little to him.
She still had an hour before he came home- if not longer- so she returned to her work. It was seven o clock before she heard his car on the drive, and saved her work hurriedly before turning off her computer and heading down. Her computer- or the computer belonging to her work was something she would still need to transport along with a few clothes, but nothing that wouldn't fit in a car.
She turned on her most charming smile and went downstairs to greet her husband. He didn't stay to exchange pleasantries or affection with her, instead heading straight to the bathroom to shower his day's work away- or the scent of Nikki. She headed into the kitchen and began preparing dinner, chicken, potatoes and salad.
Within half an hour they were sitting together at the table eating. As always, she felt as if she was treading on egg shells. He looked at her plate, half filled with salad, a chicken breast and four half potatoes. His plate held less salad and more meat and potatoes.
'Do you really want *four* potatoes?' He asked, in a neutral tone. She felt the panic rising, what had she done wrong now? 'Have you not noticed your clothing is getting rather fitting?'
'Oh, thank you darling.' She said blandly, wondering if he could sense the anger inside her. She silently placed a potato on his plate. He continued staring at her plate wordlessly, until she placed a second on his plate.
'This way you should fit into the blue dress for Friday. The one I bought you, last year.' Her heart sank, the blue dress he had bought her was very fitting and she wasn't sure it would fit. And she knew that if she didn't wear it, he would be angry afterwards, never at the time. He was always so loving, affectionate and personable in front of people. She hadn't understood how easily Claire's family could believe how he was to her, he was always so charming in front of them. She knew if she told people what had happened that night, they would never believe her. Then she smiled. There wouldn't be an afterwards this time.

'What a great idea,' she smiled at him, 'I was wondering what to wear. How thoughtful you are sorting that out for me.' She used to think he was so kind taking that worry from her, telling her what to wear and often what to order in restaurants (never things she would have chosen herself). She saw it as him educating her. Only now did she realise, the education had been control. She was groomed by him to make his perfect wife, subservient to him, inferior to him but adding to his prestige with her youth, figure, clothing, hostessing, career and choices (all carefully orchestrated by him). Even the furnishings she had bought for the house were in a style she knew he would approve of, not something she wanted or liked. She had learnt to be his puppet, or his puppy, desperate for his approval.
'And we are clear. Claire will not be staying! Think of this house-warming as networking. Our priority is my career and our standing in this village. You can see her, if you must, when you pop down to London to sort out and sell that mausoleum your gran called a home. I've got lots of plans for our money when probate is through. You might even have that baby you wanted.'
She nodded, but again, as she outwardly paid him attention she realised, if he had his way there never would be a baby. It would be a distant dream he held over her with the goal posts ever moving further and further away until she was too old for it to be feasible. He would never directly say they wouldn't have a child, just delay it each time. Already she felt guilt and had confessed the contraception weekly to the priest. But her husband insisted and she had promised to love, honour and *obey*- as he often reminded her. Her fear of divorce had kept her using the Dutch Cap apart from that one night when he hadn't given her any choice.
After dinner, he approved her furniture choices and her removal of her family mementoes which he had never liked. 'Took them to the tip, did you?' He asked.
And the lies kept coming. 'Yes, I did. Time for a new future, not the past.' She said, the second part was true enough, it was almost time for her to start her new future. A future without him.
But for now, she smiled and responded to his questions and comments. Longing for bedtime when he would turn his back to her and hide his phone from her and she too could turn her back to him and stop pretending for a few hours.

Chapter 20

Her dad arrived home at half past six, as she had expected, she had got the dinner ready to heat up in pans a few minutes before while Sheryl was upstairs. Her dad seemed pleased that dinner was nearly ready and agreeable to her reading in the garden instead of her room for the evening. Sheryl didn't seem bothered either, it was clear, they just didn't want her in their way and wanted her to help around the house but weren't bothered beyond that.

Over dinner, they discussed his dad's chances of promotion and how much he was hoping when his department head retired later this year he would be promoted to the post in an internal promotion rather than the post being advertised. Other than wishing him luck, it wasn't really a conversation she could add much too. Sheryl, as she had previously worked there too had quite a lot to add about why he would be the best candidate. He pointed out it might be harder to come and visit her as working hours would be longer.

'I'm afraid when I get that promotion it won't be possible to pop and see you in London so much. More travelling and dinners I will have to attend.'

'But even if you don't, sweetheart, we will have a family here. You can't be going to London every other weekend when you have a family at home. Once every couple of month or so.' then Sheryl smiled at her, 'And anyway, you will want to come up and help with your brother in the holidays. So really sweetheart, you won't need to go down there at all really.'

'Well, I hadn't really thought about that. But of course, my promotion will need to take priority.'

Sheryl smiled sweetly at him and frowned at her.

Prompted she replied. 'Of course, Dad.' But she couldn't help the sinking feeling in her stomach as she took in what Sheryl had hinted. She wasn't really part of their family, she was only wanted if she was prepared to be useful, not as a member of the family. She also noticed that despite having no idea what sex the baby was, Sheryl and her dad were both convinced it was a boy. They spoke about the baby as he, the nursery was being decorated in blue, boys' names being discussed and boys' clothes being picked out. She wondered idly what would happen if the eagerly anticipated he turned out to be a she. Then she smiled wryly, no need to wonder, she was living that life, unwanted by her father. She had been lucky to have been

wanted and loved by her mum and grandma. Should the new baby prove to disappoint expectations she hoped Sheryl had loving parents to help this child as nothing so far had suggested her dad or Sheryl would, and Gran would certainly not take on a child who was no kin of her own, and she would be in education for some time to come and she didn't really want to care for a sibling.
Once dinner was eaten, Sheryl and her dad left the room to have a private evening together, leaving her to clear and wash up before going outside with her book. She sat on a plastic chair and enjoyed the evening warmth as she pulled out a book. She didn't have very many books left to read that she had brought with her, she needed to ask Sheryl and her Dad if they had any she could borrow, or start rereading the ones she had already read. She had Penhallow by Georgette Heyer tonight. It was her Gran's least favourite Georgette Heyer, she never read it on her read through of Georgette Heyer. She thought the characters were barbaric. It was rare for them to disagree on books. But Wuthering Heights and Penhallow were two. Gran felt Wuthering Heights was the furthest thing from romance she had ever read and that they all acted without any morals or consideration. Gran had no time for the book. She however felt differently. She felt that circumstance had made the characters into the characters they were fighting for their survival in the only ways they knew how.
She read the first half of Penhallow sitting on the plastic chair, she could see Gran's point, the characters were hardly likeable, you wouldn't choose to go on holiday with any of them. She always thought it was strange how similar Penhallow was to Rebecca. They were written at a similar time and both were tales of a second wife living in the shadow of the first and the impact of a dreadful secret. She thought wryly about her father and his second wife. Sheryl was certainly not living in the shadow of her mum. The only shadow of her mum was her, and she was sure both her dad and Sheryl would be happy if the shadow was to disappear forever. There were no photos, no memorabilia of her mum, there wasn't even an ornament or piece of furniture she remembered from her childhood with her mother in the house. The first wife had been successfully erased here, no portrait for the second wife to gaze at in awe or trepedation, the only shadow of her existed in the daughter who was slowly being erased from their life unless it was of benefit to them. Neither her Dad or Sheryl had shown any interest in her other than how she

could help them and when she should disappear. They had told her to find other children to play with and washed their hands of her not even asking if she needed anything.
Luckily, she had found a friend, a delightful friend. Maybe the kissing meant he was her boyfriend? She knew better than to ask him, the girls at school said boys hated being asked to talk about things like that, you played it cool and let them say it. Her thoughts strayed to the day she had had with him. The kisses, him in nothing but his underwear. That had surprised her, but she had thought about it, he didn't have much money, she presumed swim wear was too expensive or hard to buy in the small town nearby. He was so good-looking and when he touched her, she wanted to pull him closer and feel his whole body against hers, but she knew to resist it. Some things had to wait until marriage.
She let Penhallow fall to her lap as she imagined being married to Jasper. It wouldn't be a big wedding of course and they'd live in a small attic flat in London, not far from Gran...
She realised the light was beginning to fail and put her chair back exactly where she had found it before gathering up her things and going indoors. She knocked briefly on the closed door to the living room and told Sheryl and her dad she was going to bed without opening the door.
In bed she fell asleep almost immediately, still thinking about the sensation of kissing Jasper and what exactly happily ever after might entail.

Chapter 21

She lay beside him in bed, she could hear his rhythmical gentle snores and feel the breeze from the open window. But she couldn't sleep.
Her heart raced as she thought of her plan to leave him. To just head back to London, to her home and live there alone. She had never lived alone. She had lived with Mum and to a lesser degree Dad, then with Gran, after marriage she had moved in with James to his flat until with her added income they had bought the small townhouse with a garage taking up most of the ground floor of the plot a few minutes from her Gran. She had stayed with Gran nursing her until her death and then afterwards, in her childhood bedroom,

dealing alone with the paperwork and effects of grief from two causes while James transferred offices and moved their home. He had spent a couple of nights a week at her Gran's house with her but had been far too busy to be around much, or help at all. He had stood beside her at the funeral, wiping her tears with a large white handkerchief, an arm protectively around her. But in private, he had had very little to say except about his plans for *their* inheritance. When his parents and grandparents had died, he had been very clear that as the pre-nup stated the money was his, not joint property. She had very little idea what exactly he inherited, except it had been far less than he envisaged and he was very bitter about it. She suspected most of it had gone on the Jaguar E type which he kept carefully under wraps in a garage near his work in London and presumably now in the garage beside their house. She realised she hadn't even ventured there yet.
While he only drove it a few times a year, and rarely with her beside him, he took great pride in pulling it onto the front for its weekly clean and comments of admiration from the neighbours.
She remembered sadly when they had started 'going out'. She was eighteen, having left school and started at university to study English at a local university, she hadn't needed to leave home. Claire and her were doing the same course, at the same university. In the same classes. Just as they had done for school, they walked together to the same tube station and caught the same line, just a few stops further along than school had been. They sat together in classes and were part of the same group of friends. They had been to an all-girls school, and other than Claire's three brothers and their friends (all younger than them) they had had very little to do with boys other than at church events. They didn't really fit in with the students their age, who were for the main part living in halls and enjoying the opportunities to party and drink away from their families. The friends they made had been older, the mature students. There were three mature students in their class. Two were women in their late twenties or thrities, who had had their families young and were taking the opportunity of their children being in school to study for their degrees with the aim of becoming Secondary School English teachers. The other was Jenny. She was twenty-three and lived with her boyfriend (something they never told their families) a few minutes from university. She had left school and taken a job as a

travel rep with Club 18-30- something else neither of their families had ever been told- and come back to education later. She described herself as partied out and had drifted away from the party group to their more focussed group. She aimed to get a First Class degree and then train to be a lawyer.
It was ironic that although she had met James at Jenny's engagement party, he had been very keen to end her friendship with Jenny, even telling her Gran that he thought Jenny was unsuitable and immoral. After they finished University and they married, it seemed meeting with Jenny always clashed with her role as his wife and they lost touch. Claire had stayed in touch with Jenny and they had met at a few life events over the years, Claire's wedding, her child's Christening and her husband's 30th but with James protectively by her side, they had just awkwardly exchanged greetings and small-talk for a few moments before moving on.
She thought about the other friends she had drifted away from over the years. Emmie had won his disapproval too. She was a feminist, a journalist specialising in women's issues. No wonder she wasn't married he always said. Lisa and Sarah, renting a house together in Battersea both teachers- closet lesbians he called them. They weren't in the closet, they had been until they left university and were still dependent on their parents, not knowing how they would react. Both sets of parents were surprised at first but no one was disowned and the six of them would stay together in Cyprus in a villa for Christmas each year. Other friends she had made at work were always unsuitable in some way too. Had it not been for Claire, she would now have been left with no one. But Claire was tenacious, and also perfectly at home walking into Gran's and putting the kettle on, just as she had been since childhood.
He had never objected to her visiting her Gran, encouraging her to spend evenings there while he was networking at work in the evenings, angling for promotion (although she now suspected the actual activities had been slightly different). Claire was often there too at Gran's. Or they'd go together the few doors down the road to Claire's parents or Grandparents, their Grandma's had gone to church and school together and were still friends. While she had spoken to him about her visits with Gran, she had never mentioned these larger visits, occasionally saying she went with Gran to visit a friend of hers without specifying who. Gran never seemed to mention it to

him either. Suddenly she felt guilty, had her lies of ommission been what ruined their relationship. While he had never banned her friendships, his disapproval was clear. Should she have cut-off these friends, would that have assured her a happy marriage?
Claire's face surfaced in her mind. Assuring her, that things would have been just the same, but with her isolated. She saw in her mind, Claire holding her that night while she cried. Putting arnica on her bruises with tears rolling down her face at the sight of her bruises. Claire slept on the pullout trundle from underneath her her bed that night, as they had so many times as children. The next day, Claire's Mum had come to the hospital with her, then Claire's Dad had taken over. Until Gran came home with her, either Claire, her parents, grandparents or siblings had been with her. When Gran came home, two weeks later she assured them they were fine, but still a few times a day someone popped in with food, for a chat, to send her to rest or with a book they thought she would enjoy. |When she protested, they brushed away her concern with the assurance this is what family did. This was a stark comparison to her Dad who by now she had not heard from for over a decade, his last Chrismas card arriving when she was nineteen. He hadn't even made it for her wedding the year before that or sent a wedding card.
Realising tears were rolling down her face, she got up and went to the bathroom to compose herself before returning to bed, offering God a silent prayer of thanks for Claire and her family before finally falling asleep.

Chapter 22

Another day in heaven. She walked down to the pond with her underwear and towel in a bag (her swim wear was underneath her clothing). He was there already, in the water, swimming. The ducks were swimming at the far end of the pond, tranquilly milling around. She hurried to leave her clothes on the blanket he had once again brought and join him in the pond.
He pulled her close and kissed her immediately, this time he pulled his whole body against hers and she could feel something she knew she shouldn't pressed up against her. She stood tensely while he kissed her at first. But he didn't seem to expect anything else, so she allowed herself to relax into his arms and kissed him back with

fervour and passion. Standing, kissing in the water, proved to be a chilly experience, so they got out to lie on the blanket together, arms wrapped around each other. Today their entire body, head to toe was against each other as they kissed and held each other. As his lower body rubbed against hers it created intensely pleasurable feelings and made her want more. She carefully pulled her lower body away from his, but soon found them against each other again and this time she didn't have the strength to pull apart, after all they were both clothed, well clothed in swimwear. It wasn't as if they were naked. Venetia certainly hadn't mentioned this in the summer idyll. She felt nervous, as though she was getting in above her head. His hand sliding to her breast cemented that thought and she disengaged, jumping up and saying it was time for a swim. Before he could respond, she was in the water, swimming, letting the cool water cool her body and ardour. She knew she had to pull away, but she hadn't wanted to. His hand on her breast had felt fantastic and she had wanted to sink into the feeling.
He lay there for a moment, watching her in the water, on his handsome face a smile. She turned to look at him, still lying there, watching her and for a moment a shiver went down her spine. It was as though for a brief moment the sun, heat and happiness had disappeared leaving this beautiful place, cold and threatening. There was no logic to the feeling, so she dismissed it but despite her happiness a shadow remained.
After a few minutes watching her, he got up and joined her in the water. More kissing and swimming races in various strokes ensued. She realised, she knew and was capable in far more strokes and definitely swam with more style, again the poverty he had grown up in showed. Whereas she had had private swimming lessons weekly until she was twelve, he had had the school lessons and swum in this pond and a nearby river without instruction. He could swim and was faster than she was, but without any particular stroke or style. He seemed to use a cross between breast stroke and doggy paddle.
Again they got out to lie on the blanket and again their bodies writhed against each other, she allowed his hands to find her breasts and lay against him savouring the feeling of him touching her and rubbing against her. She felt she could stay like that, kissing and holding and enjoying for ever, but far too soon, before even lunch time he sat up and looked at her watch.

'I have to go.' He said. 'I need to do some jobs for Ma and Nan, then I've got work a bit earlier.'
She looked at him aghast. So soon. She had hoped for a whole day here in his arms. She knew better than to say so, but she was sure he could read her feelings on her face. 'Of course. When will I see you again?' She asked nervously.
He paused for a second and leaned down to kiss her. ' Or, you could always come with me? Ma and Nan are out. No one will see us. Get a couple more hours together until I go to work.'
She nodded, grabbed her bag and went behind the tree to put her clothing back on.
They headed together up the path, which was deserted in the heat of the day.
His house was one of a row of council houses or ex council houses. The one he lived in, and the one next door which he told her his gran lived in looked run down, the others looked as thought they had been done up and extended with porches, side extensions and conservatories all visible. It was a 1930s building, with a living room, kitchen and bathroom downstairs and (he told her) two bedrooms upstairs. The living room was small holding a two seater sofa, an unmatchied wingback chair, a tiny sidetable between them with a telephone on, an old TV, and a bookcase with well used paperbacks in. Even with so little in it, it felt crowded. The kitchen was about the same size. It had a pull out table and two chairs (a folding chair was hung up behind the door) as well as the usual kitchen cupboards, fridge, cooker and sink. Everything looked old, grubby and worn. The floor in the kitchen was well-worn linoleum in a 1970s pattern of orange and brown circles. He got out two chipped glasses which he filled with tap water.
'Have a drink.' He said, drinking his own glass.
She drank her water and followed him out into the garden. There was an old and clearly mended garden shed, he opened it and pulled out a pair of gloves and a couple of garden trugs with small garden tools in. Walking down to the end of the garden, he stopped by a number of vegetable beds, which not only covered his garden but went through into his Nan's garden too. He bent over and started weeding.
'You sit on the lawn and chat to me.' he ordered.
Instead, she walked back to the shed and pulled out another pair of

gardening gloves and joined him weeding.
'My Gran grows vegetables too, weeding is my usual job.' She reassured him as she joined him pulling and digging at the bindweed growing in from the filed behind.
They worked on in companionable silence weeding all the beds but one before he stopped and said he needed to go to work. Again he kissed her and they agreed to meet at the pond the following day.

Chapter 23

She woke with a start. Usually, she was awake before him long before him and she used that time to ready herself for the day ahead. But today he was already in the shower when she woke up. She jumped out of bed, and hurried into the walk in wardrobe to find some clothes for the day. It didn't take long to dress and brush her hair quickly into a bun. She hurried downstairs to make the coffee he'd be expecting.

A few minutes later, he arrived downstairs jovial and chiding her for her late morning. She smiled sweetly at him, as she knew he expected and apologised for her tardiness. He took this in good part saying it must be the country air keeping her asleep longer. She knew in actuality it had taken her hours to fall asleep the night before. She pretended to sip her coffee while he ate a more substantial breakfast holding in the queasiness until after he had left .

As soon as he left, she hurried to the downstairs shower room and barely made it before she emptied the contents of her stomach. After cleaning herself and the bathroom to make sure no evidence was visible, she hurried upstairs to shower.

Afterwards, heading straight to her office she switched on a computer and replied to emails before starting her day's work.

For once her work didn't keep her mind occupied and she found her mind wandering back to days gone by, when she had thought they were happy.

They'd been dating for only a few months (an old-fashioned courtship her Grandma had called it) when he asked her to marry him. He had collected her two or three times a week from her Grandma's house complete with flowers for both herself and sometimes her grandma and taken her out for dinners or once to see a film he wanted to see at the cinema, and occasionally to dinner parties or parties held by his friends. Most of his friends seem to be older than him with wives of a similar age meaning she felt very out of her depth in their conversations sometimes, They all seem to have children and families and a busy social life attending events she never really heard of while she attended university (something they all smiled sweetly about but she felt they were silently laughing behind her back. None of them had attended university being a wife and being a mother was their role in life.

Knowing how much it meant to James for her to fit in with his friends, she smiled adjusted her conversation and tried to fit in. Inside she was screaming to return home. She knew she was lucky, he clearly loved her, he showered her with gifts he complimented her constantly and he was so attentive to her and he was so handsome. All of his friends wives told her told her how lucky she was, he'd never brought a woman to their gatherings before. She really was special. He too told her how special she was. How he'd never felt this way for anyone. How they were meant for each other, soulmates she had thought.

Like most 18 years old would be, or at least 18 years as innocent and naïve as her she was bowled over by his love. When only 6 months later he asked her to marry him she had no hesitation in saying yes.

Gran seemed a little surprised when she came home with an engagement ring and a fiance. She suggested they waited until she had finished university in just over 18 months. They could save for the next 18 months. Their courtship continued with James collecting her 4 or 5 times a week now and taking her to restaurants or dinners with his friends, once or twice to the theatre and to work gatherings with him. He started to explain to her how she should be dressing for things. Even taking her shopping and guiding her clothing choices- she paid for herself of course. She knew she was the luckiest girl in the world and looked forward to her future with him.

The only slight cloud on the horizon seemed to be his difficulties with Clare although he pretended there wasn't a problem it was very clear he did not like Claire. He was polite to her when he talked but it was clear he had no pleasure in the conversation and no desire to continue it. When her boyfriend, later husband, was home on leave from the Army again the same was true. Without ever saying a word against Claire it seemed to be more difficult for her to meet Claire. There were family dinners, people she must meet, or work commitments that he really needed her to attend with him. Although when they went, she was there she seemed surplus to requirements. Other than attending university together, her and Claire seemed to see less and less of each other in their free time.

The same also seemed to be true of other friends of hers. Her relationships with them seemed to deteriorate, never ending outright in an argument but they soon tired of the constant cancellations of their time together or she had difficulties finding time to spend with them as well as James. They stopped calling. They stopped inviting her to things and became acquaintances. At first she didn't really notice, she was too busy being in love and being James's fiance. It was only when it came to wedding invitations that she realized she hadn't seen these people for a year and she could no longer call them her close friends.

Her dad had come to England shortly after they were engaged and accompanied them to dinner out. Cheryl had been with them, pregnant. But they'd left her baby sister, who she'd never met, in France, where they were living. This was a second honeymoon for them so they couldn't afford to spend much time with her, they had other plans ,but at James's cost they went out to dinner one night and showed the supreme disinterest in her which had always characterized their relationship.

Her dad seemed to like and approve of James which she thought was a good sign and hoped this might be the start of a closer relationship. The lack of wedding card later that year and the ceasing of Christmas cards soon disabused her of that notion.

She barely missed them as she always had her gran.

She imagined briefly what it would be like to have been brought up by a father who was interested who did care and he took the time to spend with her and her future husband to understand what he was like and to safeguard her against future issues. Putting her work aside completely, she returned to her plan. The house was now furnished. The food was now ordered. Claire had her precious belongings and the spare key. She would ensure they would be returned safely to her house. Looking through her plan which was disguised as a work file, she put an additional note on it, locksmith Saturday morning.

Chapter 24

After such an idyllic day, and with the promise of another tomorrow, returning to Dad's house seemed not quite so bad. But getting back there soon proved that not to be the case.

Sheryl was out, but all the cups and dishes she had used that day were around the house. By the kitchen sink was a note telling me Sheryl had started cleaning the house- done their bedroom but she was to finish off.

She loaded and started the dishwasher before moving on to the cleaning. She started by hoovering the floors before she moved on to cleaning the bathroom and wiping down the kitchen surfaces. It wasn't a very thorough job but after all what did she expect from a fifteen-year-old?

When they arrived home expecting dinner to be made, she soon learnt the answer. They expected a lot more than was done. As there was almost no fresh food in the house, she had frozen fish and chips from the freezer and a tin of mushy peas in a Pan ready to go on when they got home. Both were unimpressed. Sheryl said she should know fish made her sick. Dad said she should have made more effort making something fresh. When she pointed out that there was no fresh food in the house he was unimpressed and told her to stop blaming others before berating me for my rudeness.

As there wasn't a shop in the village she wasn't old enough to drive and certainly didn't have the money to purchase food, she was not quite sure what he expected.

She was left to eat the fish and chips alone, while Dad took Sheryl out far away from the smell of fish which Sheryl claimed made her sick. She wasn't quite as convinced, having cleared up her tuna jacket potato lunch.

She ate two portions of fish and chips, starving as she hadn't had any lunch. There was no bread or sandwich fillings left by this point and no suggestion of anyone buying more.

She wrapped the remaining portion in foil and put it in the fridge, hoping it would still be there for lunch tomorrow.

She took the opportunity to ring Gran, and almost cried when she wished her a happy birthday for the following day.

They had had plans for that day, planned to go to the cinema with Clare and Emmy, then afterwards to go for pizza- a very rare treat in her life. Instead, She'd be here for her 16th birthday. she was sure dad wouldn't remember and she couldn't see Cheryl knowing. And she certainly wasn't going to sell Jasper it was her birthday, she was sure he would feel guilty for not knowing, so she doubted anybody would even say 'Happy Birthday'. Tears pricked in her eyes as she remembered Mum making her birthdays so special. The special birthday breakfasts and the cake after school or work.

She cleared up after dinner and went to sit in the garden. Maybe tomorrow, if she wasn't expected to do anything, she could walk into Fenland (although there didn't seem to be a footpath to do that) and spend money on books in a charity shop. She had £5.00 which Gran had given her early when she realised I they wouldn't be together for her birthday. Maybe she'd find a Terry Prachett or a James Herbert, or anything else. She had almost run out of books to read and there didn't seem to be any around the house, unless Sheryl kept some in their room which she wasn't allowed to enter.

Taking her final books, a well thumbed paperback of Lord Byron (her favourite poet) and Margery Allingham's Sweet Danger, she went and sat in the garden until the light faded too much to read.

Dad and Sheryl weren't back when she took herself to bed and read her chapter of Venetia. She'd turned the lights out and was lying wakeful still when she heard them come in. They headed to bed without checking on her or quietening their voices to not disturb her. She wondered if they even remembered that she was there.

Again, she felt like crying. But she held the tears in, worrying that she was becoming pathetic. Instead, she daydreamed about Damer...Jasper. She thought about Damerel in Venetia and Lord Byron, the romantic poet. Jasper was as attractive, clever and romantic as any of them. But he was real. And he liked her.

She couldn't help but hear her dad and Sheryl's usual nightly activities. It still made her uncomfortable but she realised that it would be a nightly occurrence she had no choice but to put up with.

Daringly, she wondered what it would be like to do it with Jasper. It sounded disgusting when it was explained by the headmistress in school last year for their science GCSE. All the girls had been horrified at the thought their parents had done that. Claire in particular as she realised her parents must have done it six times! Her headmistress had stressed a lot of times that it was something only married people did, and had got very embarrassed when Lucy asked how she had been born as her mother had never been married. Later, after class, Hannah had said she had done it and it wasn't disgusting but nice. Hannah had an older boyfriend her parents didn't know about. He was nineteen and rode a motorbike. He met her around the corner after school sometimes, well away from anywhere the teachers could see them together. Hannah's parents both worked, so she would tell her parents she was going to the library to study but go off with him, then go home later. She had always thought she wouldn't like someone to do that to her, but when Jasper had kissed her earlier and rubbed against her, it had felt... really, really nice and she hadn't wanted it to stop. Maybe Hannah was right and it would be nice. Sheryl seemed to be enjoying it.

Chapter 25

While he was still at work, she continued with her plans. She completed her work for the day then rang Claire at work to confirm some details. Before he reached home she took the time to change from her casual clothes into clothes he would be happy to see her in. Stepford Wife, she thought to herself wryly as she dressed. But there was no point angering him, not when everything was nearly ready.
He reached home around seven, she had dinner prepared as he expected. A simple prawn linguine, prawns in a tomato and basil sauce served over linguine with garlic bread for him, but for her no garlic bread- remembering his comments on her potatoes the night before. She was glad she had eaten a large slice of cake after her lunch today as she was sure the meagre portion of pasta she had allotted herself would not have been sufficient otherwise.
As she stirred the sauce, expecting his imminent arrival, she thought about one of her activities that day. Unlike James, she had an

excellent working knowledge of computers. In his office sat what had previously been their shared home computer. The computer she had found the e mails on. The computer now sat in his office, and she had her own space upstairs with her work computer. She had spent a considerable amount of time earlier in his office, accessing his e mails and sending some of them to herself before removing any trace of her doing that. When he was sleeping tonight, she would be doing the same with his mobile phone texts and certain photographs she suspected were on his phone.
When he came through the door, quick to disappear upstairs and into a shower, she put the pasta in the pan, and the prawns in when she heard the shower upstairs stop. By the time he came downstairs, she was serving both meals.
'I invited my boss from work.' he said without preamble, 'And his wife, so make sure everything is perfect. Afterall, I need a promotion if you are thinking about a baby. So make sure you look good in that dress for Friday..'
He tucked into his meal, scowling at her when she did the same. When he finished his meal, he poured himself and overly generous whisky and she knew whatever she did, the evening was not going to be pleasant.
'Probate. Has it come through yet? We could do with the money from the sale of the house to do this one up properly. Not yet? Well I think you'd better give me the number, see if I can chivvy them along a bit. They might listen to a man more... A year? That is ridiculous. It isn't as if she had anyone else to leave it to. Tomorrow, you give me the number and I will sort it out.'
'That dress looks a bit for fitting than it used to be around the waist. Being thirty is no excuse to let yourself go. You need to eat less and sign yourself up to an exercise class. Plenty of time now, have you handed in your notice yet? Well I really think it is time you did. You can take that ridiculous computer back to them then and I could have that room as a dressing room. If you aren't going to do it, I might have to do it for you. What do you mean I **can't** do that? **I** am your husband. You **will** take that ridiculous computer back tomorrow and tell them you will no longer be working for them, do you **understand**?'
'The bloody waterworks. Such a manipulative woman you turned out to be. I gently point out you've let yourself go and try to help keep

you from being overworked and what do you do? Cry at me. Bloody pathetic! I saw the way Claire's family looked at me, told them lies about me have you? How I mistreat you? I wonder what they and your priest would think about a wife who breaks her wedding vows, disobeying her husband at every turn.'
Suddenly his hand reached out and grabbed her hair. He pulled her close and looked in her eyes. ' don't you be forgetting those wedding vows my *obedient* little wife. You'd be *nothing* without me. Still sleeping in your Gran's attic room a *virgin* forever.' He pulled her closer and kissed her roughly. 'Frigid bitch!' He slurred when she didn't respond. Then he threw his glass at the wall, whisky and glass flew everywhere, some hitting her and cutting her cheek.
'Clear that up!' He shouted as he got up and staggered off to bed.
She fled to the downstairs shower room, where after a glance in the mirror at the blood now dripping down her cheek, she threw up from a mixture of shock and the taste of his whisky in her mouth. He was always verbally aggressive after whisky, although she didn't find that out until a few years into the marriage when he started drinking whisky (which he had always avoided before), calling her names and laughing at her frigidity and mocking her appearance but the physical violence was new. That had begun that awful night, the night she saw the e mails and Gran...
He had visited her when she was nursing Gran, he had been so contrite and apologetic. She had truly believed him when he said it would never happen again, after all, it hadn't happened in ten years so she believed him, didn't she see that it was a moment of madness, never to be repeated? Soon he had convinced her that it was her fault for snooping. He didn't go as far as telling her she had deserved it, but the blame was certainly at least evenly distributed.
But now, his moments of madness seemed to be becoming for frequent.
She cleaned up herself, before cleaning up the glass and whisky from the living room. She hoovered three times before she thought she had all the slivers of glass.
Not wanting to join him upstairs, where she could hear him snoring, she contemplated sleeping on the sofa, but knew that would just be the cause of tomorrow's argument, so reluctantly made her way up the stairs to their bedroom.

Chapter 26

The morning did not start well. She made her way downstairs and made the coffee for her dad and Sheryl while helping herself to a glass of water. As her dad came downstairs, the phone rang. He answered it and called her immediately. It was Gran wishing her a happy birthday and telling her she loved and missed her. Tears pricked at her eyes as she thanked her Gran. She wished she was with Gran.

Walking through to the kitchen, she saw Sheryl had now joined Dad and was looking very annoyed. Before she could say anything Sheryl told her how inconsiderate it was for people to call that early when she was trying to sleep through morning sickness. She apologised.

'what was so important for *her* to call at that time anyway?' Her Dad asked.

'Just wishing me a happy birthday.' she replied.

For a brief moment her Dad looked guilty, then he blustered, 'You're too old to celebrate those anyway.' and went back to his coffee.

'I was hoping to go into Fenland Market today.' She said hopefully. 'I wanted to buy a book.'

'I'm not taking you.' Said Sheryl, heading out the kitchen and back upstairs.

'I've got work.' Said her Dad, heading out the kitchen too. 'If you can get there on bus or something, do what you want.'

After clearing the cups from the table, she wandered into the garden, not really knowing how to organise her trip to Fenland Market- she wasn't even sure which direction it was in! She stood by the gate to the footpath staring into the distance, only to jump as it opened. Jasper walked through the gate and pulled her out onto the footpath. Beside him, he had his bike.

'I need to go into Fenland Market this morning. Do you feel like coming?' He asked.

Nodding she replied, 'Yes, but how will we get there? I don't have a bike up here.'

'You sit on my handlebars.' He replied.

For a moment she was aghast. She had seen teenagers in the park doing that, but she had never tried it. But she wanted to be with Jasper and she wanted to go to town. So throwing caution to the wind,she agreed. Fifteen minutes later, after a very fast shower,

dressing in jeans and a t shirt and grabbing her purse with the book token and precious £5 note and a bit of change in, she was back and ready to go. Sitting on his handlebars took some practice and she was very glad the road was quiet as they weaved about a bit as he got used to steering with her extra weight at the front.
Fenland Market was how he had described it. A single road with a row of shops. A butcher, a baker's , a small supermarket, a few charity shops and a couple of clothes and shoe shops. A DIY store and a printer's shop with a couple of banks or building societies and estate agents too, not an exciting town for a teenager.
After locking up his bike, they went into the DIY shop where Jasper purchased some things before looking around the charity shops together at the books. She was thrilled to come out with six books, each for twenty pence, meaning her five pound note was still intact and she still had a pound in coins.
'Let's go to the bakers,' she said. 'I'll treat us both to something.'
With her remaining pound she bought them each a belgian bun.
Happy Birthday to me , she thought as they sat together on a bench, his arm around her, eating their buns. She leaned against him, feeling the warmth of his body through his t shirt, silent and comfortable.
Occasionally people walked by, smiling at them but Jasper turned resolutely away from them, and she felt to awkward to respond.
After their buns, they both were thirsty and returned to his bike where they shared the sports bottle of water he kept on his bike.
Heading back, in the same manner as they had come, she felt a sense of safety steal over her that she had not felt since her Dad had arrived at her Gran's unexpectedly to collect her for the summer.
She expected that he would head to the secluded pond, which she thought of as their special place. But to her surprise, he rode to his house and took her inside with him. His mother was in the kitchen, making herself a late breakfast before heading off to work. She looked far from pleased to see he had someone with him and while she was sat on their tiny sofa with another glass of water, his mum closed the door to the kitchen and she could hear the the whisper shouts of their conversation but not the words spoken.
Feeling incredibly awkward, she considered just heading out the front door, rather than be an unwitting ear in their disagreement- which she was sure was about her. But the television was positioned in front of the front door- she was already aware that they only used

the back door- meaning any exit from that door would be very difficult. Following a small squeal, Jasper came back into the room he had left her in and said his mum had gone to work and said to say goodbye to her and that she would see her again. A bit confused by quite what had happened, she sat beside him on the sofa watching afternoon TV and kissing while outside, for the first time since she had arrived, it rained.
They were so engrossed in their kissing and his hands wandering up her shirt that neither of them heard the kitchen door open and close until a voice called out.
'Jasper, sweetheart. Have you had any lunch? I've got some leftov....' the elderly woman stopped on the threshold to the room as she saw them readjusting their clothes. She showed no embarrassment but continued, 'Ive got enough for both of you if you would like to join us, I'm Jasper's Nan, you can call me Mary.'
Two minutes later, she found herself sat at a tiny table in an identical kitchen to the one at jasper's house. His Nan was frying bubble and Squeak in a huge frying pan while bacon sizzled on the grill above. Mary chattered away as she cooked, telling her about the village and asking questions about her life. She found herself telling about Gran, and Mum, and then Dad and Sheryl and finally her birthday while they were eating the only meal she hadn't cooked since she left her Gran's. It was delicious.
After dinner, she washed the dishes while Mary dried and put them away and Jasper disappeared outside to do a 'quick job'. She presumed he wanted to avoid the washing up. Ten minutes later he reappeared as they finished the washing up with a small bouquet of wildflowers which he presented her with.
'Happy Birthday.' He said, kissing her as he presented her with the flowers. Her eyes filled with tears as she looked at the flowers and him.
Thanking his Nan for lunch, they left the house and the rain having stopped, walked hand in hand to the pond together. Jasper seemed to have stopped caring who saw them, and she was too infatuated to even consider caring if they were seen together.

Chapter 27

She woke in the morning as the sun came up. She knew she had at least two hours before he stirred. She quietly slipped from bed and took his phone from the bedside table beside him. Heading into the dressing room, she got to work. She took his memory card from his phone and copied the data from it onto the spare phone she had bought for the purpose. Making sure she left no evidence of her 'snooping' on his phone, she returned his phone to his bedside table, switched off her new phone and hid it behind her clothing while she showered and dressed.

Slipping the phone in her pocket, she ran lightly down the stairs. Suddenly she remembered another morning she ran lightly down the stairs, these stairs. A day she began filled with hope that ended with heartbreak. Her heart flip-flopped in her chest and she struggled to breathe. Only to Gran and the Doctor had she told part of that story. Her Dad must have guessed, at least part of it but he had never asked, or even asked how she was. His concern was elsewhere.

She contrasted in her head, her Dad's lack of concern with Gran and this time Claire. She didn't even try to excuse James in her head. Flashbacks to a traumatic event were not a good sign, she might not be a psychologist, but even she knew that. Resolutely she breathed through the memory and the one that followed just three months ago. Without realising, she stroked her belly gently.

As always, she made coffee, and a tea for herself. The smell of the coffee made her nausea rise, and she visited the downstairs shower room and got rid of all evidence long before James surfaced, running a few minutes late for work and looking terrible.

'I think I have flu. If they didn't need me so much at work, I'd stay home.'

Panic rose in her chest. She needed him to go to work for her plan. She knew this was the preamble to him making her convince him to stay home. But she couldn't do that today, so she took a daring and foolish route.

'You're hungover.' she said unsympathetically. 'Take some paracetamol.'

'I'm not hungover. Shows how much you care for me. Just a meal ticket aren't I.' He said crossly.

Inwardly, she scoffed. The meal ticket who earned less than her and contributed nothing to their joint finances.

'Well since my loving wife would rather I work myself to death, I'd better get going.' He stared at her, waiting for her to back track. When she didn't answer, he continued. 'You really would like to get your hands on my money.' When she still didn't answer, he grabbed her arm and pulled he close menacingly. As she cringed away from him, she pulled back and he pulled her closer his hand gripped her arm so she gasped.
'I'll scream and the neighbours will hear.' She said softly.
He let go of her roughly, throwing her across the room, and walking out the door.
'Hopefully, my loving wife will be in a better mood when I get home from work.' He said angrily as he walked away. 'and I expect you to be taking that computer back to London and handing in your notice today- or I will...' He slammed the door behind him and she heard him shouting jovial hellos with the neighbours and reminding them of the party the following night.
With relief she walked to the front door and looked through the window feeling relief at the sight of his car speeding up to the main road at the end of the village.
She walked upstairs and obediently unplugged and packed up her computer, taking it down the stairs and placing it by the front door. She looked at the empty boxes beside her book shelves and packed the precious books back in the boxes before carrying them down too. She returned to their bedroom and looked through her clothing. In a couple of weekend bags, she packed all the clothes she liked, mainly her casual clothes. Leaving the dresses James had chosen or approved, she took very little. She took those downstairs too to join the growing pile by the door.
Looking to make sure no neighbours were there, she started taking the boxes to her Ka. For the first time ever, she wished her car was larger, but somehow she managed to squeeze everything inside.
Once again she drove to the car park she had previously met Claire in. This time not just Claire but her husband was there too. He made fast work of emptying her car into the cavernous boot of his large estate car while Claire exclaimed in horror at the cut on her face and the bruising coming up fast on her arm- as well as the now fading bruising from previously.
Claire pulled out a digital camera and started photographing her face and arms. Her husband having finished loading the car came to join

them and as he saw her closely for the first time a look of horror came over his face, fast followed by a look of uncontrollable rage which she had never seen before.
'You aren't going back. He is escalating. He could kill you. I'm not letting that happen. And Claire, your parents would kill us if they knew we left her here.'
'He is right. We can't leave you here.' Claire said seeing the argument in her face.
'But if I just leave, he will never let me go. He will make my life hell. I have to go through with this, I have to publicly out him as an adulterer and abuser or even the priest will support him.' She argued.
He thought for a moment before he spoke. 'You drive down to your Gran's today. You call him at work towards the end of the day, saying it is taking longer to sort out the paperwork and you need to see the solicitor about your Gran's house tomorrow so you'll stay here tonight and be back to organise the party tomorrow lunchtime. We'll come up with you- in my car- yours is going to conveniently not start tomorrow. He won't come home early to help you set up. We will help you set up. We will be there when he gets back. We know he wont try anything with us all there, never does in public and won't start anything with me and Claire's brothers there. Then the plan can go as you organised, but with you safe.'
She opened her mouth to object, but Claire agreed with her husband and had taken the car keys from her hand, saying, 'I'll drive, you look terrible.'

Chapter 28

The mid-afternoon was idyllic. They walked together hand in hand through the village and past the two girls with their horses. The girls stopped and stared as they walked past together, but she didn't care. She felt so proud to be his... well what was she? His girlfriend? She hoped so... She could imagine Claire's face if she saw Jasper. She would be so happy for her!Her Gran would be too. She said once that the description of Damerel had reminded her of Grandad although he hadn't been anywhere near as well-read.
They walked down to their pond and sat beside each other on the log kissing and talking. Once again Jasper had brought a blanket which they spread out and lay on, kissing and talking. His hands wandered up her shirt and she made no attempt to stop him. She couldn't

imagine a more exciting way to spend her sixteenth birthday.
They talked and she learnt more about his life growing up in the village. His Nan had brought up his mum alone, living with her mum and dad until they died a few years ago. His mum had been a teenager when she got pregnant, his Dad was older. He had worked at the sugar beet factory with her. They'd lived together in the house he grew up in but his Dad drank a lot and he left when Jasper was five. She had never really known families where people split up. Her Catholic upbringing had been catholic in every sense of the word, the school was selective about its pupils and her Gran selective about her friendships. For the most part, her friends were the children of grandchildren of her Gran's or mum's friends who all lived a similar life and she hadn't really spent time with anyone outside what she now realised were very narrow confines.
His life didn't sound much fun. He had been bullied at school, excluded by the other children and provoked by them. While he did well at school, he always knew there was no hope of university as even with a grant, he couldn't afford to go, and his presence was needed to help out around the houses- a fact he resented bitterly.
Her heart sang when he referred to her as his girlfriend. He seemed to think she was here permanently now. She couldn't bare to correct him on this. But even with the excitement of having a boyfriend, her heart sank at the idea of having to stay indefinitely with her Dad and Sheryl. She longed for the safety of Gran's house.
She too shared her life. She told him, what she had never told anyone, not even Gran or Claire. She told him about Mum's diaries. She told him about what Mum had written about Dad and the different women over the years, and Sheryl being mentioned a lot from the year before Mum died so unexpectedly in a road traffic accident. They never had found the speeding car which hit her. She couldn't imagine living the rest of your life knowing you had killed someone but never owning up to it. Mum's death had ruined her childhood. Gran had aged overnight, she suddenly found it harder to keep up, seemed frailer and less certain of anything. Only Dad seemed unaffected. Of course he looked devastated at the funeral, where he hugged her and Gran close, but the next day he had left for work and slowly drifted away from her life. It was far more settled for her to stay with Gran he started by saying, soon they needed to help empty the house as he was selling for a more manageable flat

near his work, then gradually his presence dwindled and then he remarried- to Sheryl- and became a very minor monthly- if that- visitor in her life who never had more than a couple of hours.
She told Jasper about Claire, and Emmie, and Lucy. About their trips to the cinema, to the park, the planned pizza dinner and the school daytrip they had been on to the trenches in France. Her first and only time abroad. Gran had never been abroad, nor had Jasper- he'd never even been to London. There had been school trips both to London and abroad, but his family couldn't afford them.
At about four, they walked back to the village, Jasper needed to head to work and she needed to head back to cook dinner- if there was food in the house. They kissed a final time near the horses' field and she turned to head back down the footpath towards her Dad's house.
After a couple of minutes, she could hear running footsteps behind her and she turned half-expecting to see Jasper having come for another kiss. But instead, there stood one of the girls from the horses, looking nervous.
'I know you don't know me. But I had to talk to you.'
She smiled for a moment thinking maybe the girls with the horse wanted to make friends. But the worried look on the girl's face somehow told her that wasn't the case before the girl continued.
'Jasper. I saw you holding hands and kissing him.'
She bristled inwardly, was this one of his classmates who made his childhood friendless coming to lie about him?
'He isn't as nice as he seems. He isn't as honest as you think. Just be careful.' The girl tailed off, not really sure what to say next.
'He seems nice to me.' was all she could think to answer in the moment, hearing how silly it sounded as it came out of her mouth.
'He would. At first. He went out with my sister a few months ago. She thought he was nice too. At first...' Again she tailed off, seemingly lost for words.
'Thank you.' She said in a chilly tone.
'Well, I warned you. My sister said not to because you'd tell him. Please don't.' she looked pleadingly.
'Why shouldn't I tell him?'
'I can't explain.' She gave her a final look before heading back off towards the horses.
Confused, she continued towards her Dad's house.

Chapter 29

Sitting in the car beside Claire, she felt a peace she hadn't felt for a long time. Being comfortable together, they didn't feel the need to talk and she just let her mind wander.

I will be escaping soon, she kept thinking. I will be safe soon...

She had all the evidence she needed to prove what he had done to her hopefully enough to get a restraining order and stop him from harassing her -as she knew he would if he was allowed to do so.

She glanced at Claire, so thankful for their friendship. Not just Claire but Claire's entire family, her husband, her brothers, her sisters and her parents. All of them were helping her to leave James.

When she got to London, Claire's mum would take all the evidence they had collected to the print shop her sister ran. There would be a number of copies of the collated books- some for evidence and the rest... she smiled to herself.

She thought back to all the church services she sat through with them. All the times they were told marriage was sacred. All the teachings in the Bible of a wife obeying her husband. And she was thankful once again, that her friends will willing to see past the simple teachings and see that abuse was never acceptable.

With a right hand she lifted slightly the sleeve on her left side. It was painful to touch the skin. The bruises were black and angry. The same was true in the other side. She thought her cheek might need stitching too.

She glanced again at Clare, Claire had married a good man. A man who supported her in every endeavour and had become an integral part of the large happy family Claire was blessed with, a family who had always counted her as family too.

Part of her would like to feel sorry for herself, why had her marriage gone so terribly wrong? But in her heart she knew the answer to that. Her up bringing had been too sheltered. Her Grandma had loved her but had not been worldly enough to understand when she was being groomed by an older man who didn't really love her. He loved her youth, the image of having a young beautiful wife who others would envy him for, who he thought he appeared to be with her beside him. He wanted a young acquiescent wife. Not a real person who changed, aged and had desires of her own.

The first five years of their marriage had been idyllic. She had loved living in the flat and then the small town house together. She walked to work each morning, just a few roads away, and came home at

night to cook them a meal which would be ready to be served when James got home. With two incomes and no children, they always seemed to have the money to go out or have a couple of holidays a year.
James worked late a couple of nights a week- usually a Tuesday and Thursday- and she would go to join Gran for dinner after work, sometimes they would walk down the road to join Claire's family, and sometimes it would be just the two of them. On Sundays, James and her would go together to either Gran's or to his parents for a traditional Sunday Roast.
Her twenty-fifth birthday was the first time she had done something really wrong. They had had dinner at Gran's, Claire's family had also been there and it had been a fun, loud party. Claire's Dad had raised a glass and made a speech saying how proud he was of his 'extra daughter' and how watching her grow and mature into the intelligent woman she now was had been an honour and that Gran and her should never feel they had no family, as they were their family. Claire's youngest brother had cut the sentimentality by proclaiming she was so mature he could see the first grey hairs, and everyone except James had laughed, toasting her. James had seemed annoyed by something, and later when he joined Claire's Dad, husband and brothers, he had chosen to drink the Irish Whiskey he usually refused. She had learnt in the next few years, that that just made it worse and it was faster if she just apologised (even if in her heart she didn't really understand).
The next morning he had been abjectly apologetic, but by the following week, he had slowly changed the narrative and she was apologising for upsetting him so much, for letting him down.
It didn't happen again for a long time, months, but each time, the gap between his drunken outbursts became less until it was weekly, and he had convinced her that it was all her fault. But he never became physical, so she didn't even see it as abuse until Claire pointed it out after *that* night.
In public he was always attentive. The very picture of the besotted older husband. Everyone cooed over how he doted on her. He held her hand, opened doors, complimented her, told everyone how lucky he was. Behind closed doors it had changed. When he noticed her, he was dismissive or impatient. He seemed to work late more and

more. He was critical of her appearance and everything else. She became nervous and was constantly worried she would anger him. Her nervousness became apparent, and he publicly put it down to overwork. She was far too devoted to her job, and he did worry about her overworking. In actuality, her job was what supported them for the most part, as he contributed less and less to the bills.
She looked up, 'I need to go to the bank.' She said. 'I need to stop my salary into our joint account before next payday, it pays all the household bills on the house he bought... in his name only.'
Claire looked shocked. 'He wanted you to sell your home, to finance upgrades on a house you don't own and because of the pre-nup (if it was upheld) would have no claim over in the event of divorce?'
She nodded wryly.
'I also need to go to work. I know you explained, but I think I should too. I know you said they were happy for me to return to working in the office three days a week, home two, but I feel I owe them an explanation for all this.'
The relapsed into a comfortable silence as they continued down the motorway.

Chapter 30

She dismissed the conversation with the horse girl. Jealousy? Shhe continued towards her Dad's. She tried to quell the disquieting of her mind, but it remained as a slight shadow on her happiness. The closer to her Dad's she came that shadow in her mind receded and the shadow of what she was returning to grew bigger. She knew she would need to tidy and prepare dinner, but she wondered what else would be awaiting her.
The answer was an empty house... there was a note saying to make herself dinner (looking round and realising no one had done shopping, she wondered what exactly she was meant to make dinner with?) or, if she had the money there was a chip van that came at five. Looking at her watch, she realised she had time to do that, and luckily the money for a bag of chips. Sheryl had gone to meet her Dad. The irony of being left alone on her birthday after he had been so determined to bring her back here with him despite her birthday plans was not lost on her. She could not help but think badly of him for his total unconcern for her and their attempts to use her as an unpaid house help.

She imagined being at home with Gran and the cinema trip and birthday cake after pizza. It felt most unfair.
She noticed the post sitting on the table and glancing, saw there were envelopes addressed to her...
Taking them, she opened them to find cards, a card from gran, from Claire, her siblings and parents, another from Claire's grandparents, one from Emmie and another from some of the ladies at church who were friends with her gran. The first four all included a note saying her presents were waiting at home for her, but the final one included the five pound note which the ladies from church always clubbed together to give her. Suddenly, she had a wonderful idea, she had ten pounds, surely that would be enough for a ticket to London.
Then she remembered Jasper. How could she leave him? Maybe he could come too. The church notice board often had rooms for rent advertised on it. Several of the older couples rented out a room to students or young workers now their children had left home and they had retired, to give them a little bit more income. Maybe she could go home and secure him a room, then he could come down too? He was as desperate to get away as she was- for very different reasons. Tomorrow, she would talk to him...
She looked in the freezer and saw a single portion of frozen cod in parsley sauce and there was a bendy carrot in the veg drawer in the fridge. She decided she would buy herself a bag of chips and cook those to go with it, they could both be boiled in the same pan.
Looking at the kitchen clock, she gathered her things to walk down and find the chip van- she presumed it would be outside the church or by the bus stop.
She quickly spied the chip van, it stopped in the middle of the main road, not far from her Dad's house. A small bag of chips was 30p, which used up pretty much the last of her change, leaving her with only 3p in change, but she was so hungry she didn't care as long as the precious five pound notes were intact.
As she turned away from the van, she saw the two horse girls walking towards her, she automatically smiled. The one who had spoken to her earlier, gave her a dirty look, the other looked away from her. Sighing, she walked towards her Dad's house, ready for another lonely evening.
Getting in she ate her chips while her cod and carrot cooked, then ate them as a second course. She decided to put her rubbish straight into

the outside bin, so Sheryl couldn't moan about the smell, and opened the doors to air out the house for the same reason.
After clearing up, and making sure the house was clean and tidy, she put her shopping from earlier upstairs. Looking at the wind and drizzle, she closed the doors and decided to read indoors. Glancing at the book, she had left downstairs from her shopping earlier, she opened it and started reading.
It was a very well read Nancy Drew book, but one she hadn't read. Password to Larkspur Lane, had her enthralled and she did not look up again until she had finished reading it only two hours later. She swapped it over with the other Nancy Drew book she had picked up- another she had not read- this time from the Nancy Drew Files series- Stay Tuned for Danger, and the next time she looked up, it was a few minutes before ten and she thought she should go to bed, ready to share her ideas with Dam- Jasper tomorrow.
She had been in bed about thirty minutes when she heard her Dad and Sheryl arrive home. As usual, they made no attempt to be quiet. This cemented in her mind her determination to return home, even if Jasper didn't want to move to London.
She would leave a note for her Dad and hopefully as she was sixteen now, he wouldn't come down and make her return. He clearly didn't actually want her there apart from her being useful. Maybe she should stop being useful? And just brave the anger of Sheryl and her dad. That way he wouldn't want her back here again.
For a moment she imagined disappearing now, in the night while they slept, but she was pretty sure there were no trains at night. He would ring Gran and then she would worry, whereas if she left when he thought she was out walking around the village, she could arrive safely before he even knew she was gone. She really didn't want Gran to worry. Plus she needed to tell Jasper and see if he would come too.
Her planning didn't get any further as nature took over and she fell asleep.

Chapter 31

She had sat in the car making a mental checklist. The bank- change the direct debit from her personal account to the joint one. Remove her name from the joint account. Remove her name from the joint savings account- although she didn't think there was much-if anything- in it. James had all but emptied it buying things for *his* new house. Go into work and explain the situation. Tell them from Monday she would be available to work in the office again. Change the locks on the doors to Grans- *her* house (a stab of pain went through her every time she remembered Gran would never again be with her in their home). Maybe see about some sort of home and car security. She had made sure she took the spare key to her home and she didn't think James had keys to her home, but she believed in being careful.

After unpacking the boxes she had brought in her car and completing some of the jobs on her list and making appointments for the following day with both her solicitor and the bank, then she steeled herself to ring him.

'James' darling,' (she tasted sick in her mouth saying that, but she had rung him on his work line so he couldn't berate her and she had to keep up the act for one more day) 'I need to see the solicitor about sorting the house tomorrow and it is a long drive back, so I'm going to stay overnight and start with boxes at the house (all true, he didn't know she was unpacking boxes of books she had brought back with her rather than packing boxes)... 'of course I'll be back for the party, I'll drive straight up after the solicitors and set it all up, you don't need to worry... ...I hope you are feeling better now, this way you can get some rest... ...Love you too, will see you tomorrow.'

She put the phone down and glanced up to see Claire standing in the doorway to the room with one of her brothers. They had refused to let her be alone in case James decided to come down to London.

'Well that choked me, hearing you say that.' Claire commented wryly.

'Hope *he* chokes!' Her brother Sean barked. 'I called in at the chip shop on the way here, Claire plated up while you were on the phone.'

She was filled with a feeling of warmth, despite the loss of Gran and the imminent divorce, she had a family who loved her even if they didn't share blood.

Downstairs, the table held not just fish and chips but a large cardboard box which hadn't been there before. Sean and Claire would not let her look in it until dinner was eaten and cleared away. Inside the box were small A5 books entitled 'The story of Us'. The books started in the expected way with photos of a young couple and

captions explaining where the photos were taken. The party they met at, their first date, their engagement, their wedding, anniversaries etc. Then the photos took a sordid turn with photos of him and Lisa kissing intimately (nothing indecent had been included) and on a hotel bed clothed but with discarded articles visible which made it clear they had spent the night together. Then the photos of her bruises. The x-rays, the medical reports. The photo of her bruised and battered by her Gran's bedside. The e mails showing where and how he had spent the night. The story of us moved from a love story to a story of abuse and infidelity. The story of us was not how James wanted the world to see him.
She spent a long time looking through the book, silently reliving every memory. The hope and happiness to the pain and despair. She traced each bruise in each photo and remembered how they had arrived on her and the words which had accompanied them. Claire and Sean sat silently beside her as she relived her life. A strangled sob broke from her as she looked at the photo of her beside her Gran's bed, her gran hardly visible beneath the wires and medical equipment, her hardly recognisable underneath the bruising. Claire pulled her chair closer and leaned against her, resting a hand on her shoulder, beside her, reassuring her as she had always done.
When, at last, she had finished looking through the book, she stood and thanked them. Sean especially as it had been he and his mother who had printed these books through their printing firm and were refusing to be paid for it. He pulled her into a hug, and whispered, his voice choked with emotion.
'That bastard won't be touching you again. I promise.'
Looking through tears between them, for the first time, she truly believed that really was the case. Until now, she had been scared her preparation was not enough and he would come after her.

Taking a copy of the book and a folder Claire had placed next to the box, she told them that in two days she would be going to the police to ask them to press charges of domestic abuse, as they had been urging her to do.

Together, her and Claire went upstairs to bed. Sean saying he would rather sleep downstairs on the sofa- just in case.

Chapter 32

Remembering her resolve the previous night, she headed out without clearing up the debris from her dad or Sheryl's breakfast.. She refused to leave hers dirty, Gran had taught her better than that. But she didn't clear up after them!
Heading out, she debated whether or not she should walk to their pond or to his house. His family clearly knew about her, but could she face knocking on his door and seeing his mother or grandmother? She decided to brave it and knock on his door...
His mother answered and invited her in, he was still dressing, so she stood awkwardly in the kitchen making small-talk with his mum. She was handed a cup of tea as she awkwardly answered questions and tried to think of things to say. She couldn't help but notice the bruises on her mum's face arms and neck. She wondered how she had the bruises, but knew better than to ask. She didn't think she could say much more about the weather by the time Jasper came downstairs.
His mother took her tea and went into the living room leaving them in the kitchen. She noticed his mother flinching as he walked past her and thought what a nervous woman she seemed to be. He kissed her but it felt awkward with his mum on the other side of a thin wall. Understanding her discomfort he called to his mum that they were going out and they walked together through the footpaths to their pond.
She avoided the conversation she was waiting for and instead asked him how his mum had so many bruises, had she been in an accident? He told her about the car crash his mum had been in a couple of weeks ago. She had done a first aid at Guides and the colour of the bruises didn't quite fit with his timeline, and she seemed more bruised today than yesterday. Maybe his mum was clumsy and had fallen over since and didn't want to tell him. Claire's family always laughed about how unobservant her dad was. Her mum had cut her hair short a few months ago and he hadn't noticed for two days. Maybe Jasper was just as unobservant. She smiled remembering them all laughing when Claire's dad had suddenly noticed, half way through Sunday dinner- which Gran and her always joined them for after church. Gran always made the pudding, and Claire and her helped Claire's mum and the grans prepare the veg, her younger sisters laid the table and sorted the seats, the boys and Claire's Dad chopped wood while they prepared dinner- enough for her Gran as

well- and did any odd jobs. Claire's Grandad was in charge of stacking the wood, he stacked Gran's too. Her Dad suddenly noticed as her mum was leaning across and serving vegetables to her youngest brother, who tended to drop them. Everyone had laughed that he only noticed her Friday night haircut on Sunday. He was very red-faced laughing at himself too. The boys probably wouldn't have noticed either if they hadn't been there while it was happening.
They walked past the two horse girls again, she was unsurprised when both turned away from them as they passed, until that moment she had forgotten the strange conversation with one of them the day before. She was tempted to mention it to Jasper but decided not to, as she had other more important things to discuss and didn't think silly rumours would do anything but sadden him. They were probably like a certain couple of girls at her school, who weren't entirely truthful and could be counted on to exaggerate or make up things about other girls. They had said such unkind things about Jane when she put some weight on. Jane had suddenly left school at Easter, and not come back to do her GCSE's. Claire had seen her at the doctors and said she had put on even more weight but Jane's mum hurried her away before they could talk.
When they reached the pond, she couldn't start to tell him straight away, first they had put down the blanket and kissed. Kissing Jasper had taken everything else from her mind and she had lived in the moment. They lay together on the blanket, arms wrapped around each other, kissing and giggling over very little, enjoying each other's company. The kisses became more passionate and Jasper's hands slipped under her loose t shirt and started once again to caress her breasts. She no longer felt awkward at his hands exploring her upper body and she too slipped a hand up his t shirt, which while generally considered far less intimate than his touching of her in that area felt incredibly daring to her.
Like most men of his age, while his body had started to grow chest hair- mainly around the nipples and some tufts on his upper chest, he was not yet covered in hair over all his chest, as he probably would be a few years hence.
Eventually, smiling, she pulled away from him and the exciting sensation of this form of intimacy with him.
'Can we talk?' she started, and she saw him freeze. For a moment, a look of fear and possibly anger came over his face.

'Talk?' He said in an attempt at an even tone. 'This doesn't sound good.' a frown puckered his brow.
Leaving out her conversation with the horse girl yesterday, she told him about her experiences with her dad and Sheryl since arriving in the village- the lack of even a birthday card or wishes. The household chores, the lack of food options to cook, the criticism, being ignored and how much she missed her Gran.
Feeling the words were flowing easily now, she moved onto her plan...
Her ten pounds- she felt so rich- the train to London. Returning to the safety of Gran, the haven of Gran. Finding a room for him to rent, a job and him coming down too. The start of a new life for them after she finishes education.
She looked at him, hoping he would love this plan as much as she did. She reached for his hand and leaned in ready to kiss him as she finished speaking.
His face didn't have the expression she had hoped for. He looked blank at first, and then she saw the expression slowly appear on his face...

Chapter 33

She travelled back to his house in the car with Claire and her husband. She dozed in the back seat while his car quickly ate up the miles. Behind their car were three more cars holding Claire's parents and siblings. Her sister and two sister in laws had stayed behind to look after the children, but all the brothers and brother in laws- including her policeman brother and lawyer brother-in-law were there. And all their boots were empty to take away anything else she wanted. With their support, she felt confident and safe.
At the house, they insisted on packing every stitch of her clothing and anything she felt any fondness for- there was very little. They wouldn't allow her to lift a finger and tidied the house for the party while she copied and deleted files from the computer. Sean was vocal in his disgust that James hadn't tided away after himself last night leaving not only dinner pans and dishes for two but also a used condom on the floor by the kitchen sofa. Conor said nothing, but his face looked grim. That too was photographed and would be printed

and added to the folder before the next visit to the solicitor about the divorce papers which would be left for James that night.
The house was quickly readied for the party and by the time James came home (not early to help- I fact barely thirty minutes before the time guest had been told) the cold food was out and the barbecue ready to be lit- so James could grill the prepared meat and take compliments.
James was not happy when he walked through the door. He had recognised Claire's car on the driveway and had plastered a false smile on his face.
'Wonderful to see you both.' a handshake and an air kiss. 'Darling, your car?'
Claire interupted, 'It wouldn't start this morning. No surprise at the age it is! So we thought we'd bring her up here rather than wait for the AA. That way *we* could help her.'
James turned red at the unexpected jibe. But before he could reply, the rest of the family had entered the hallway to greet him.
'I'm going to get ready. Are my clothes organised?' He asked.
'On the bed.' She replied, having no desire for him to realise the wardrobe was now empty of her clothes.
Unable to think of a way to separate her, he frowned and headed upstairs after throwing out a general greeting.
By the time he came downstairs guests were starting to arrive and he decided to deal with her disobedience- he had made it very clear he had not wanted Claire or her family invited- after the party, when everyone had gone home.
James was a genial host, *his* guests felt the glowing warmth of his personality and smiled in response to his sparkling wit and bonhomie. The food and drinks she had so expertly organised flowed and James headed outside with some of the powerful men from his work he was courting for a promotion and some of the 'right sort' of male neighbours he had invited to set the scene. The area by the barbecue was soon filled with male talk and laughter. All in all, James was very pleased with how the party was going and felt quite hopeful about his much needed promotion.

Inside the party was going just as swimmingly. The wives of James' powerful men and the 'right sort' of villagers were charmed by the gentlemen of Claire's family who had decided to wait upon the ladies and be charming. Only one woman stood slightly to the side. Lisa, the wife of James' manager, his colleague and so much more, was not enjoying this show of marital harmony. She had not wanted to be there, had tried pleading a headache but her husband had been insistent. She stood slightly to the side now, not taking part in the general conversation and snubbing anyone who tried to engage with her.

Most of the people outside were listening to a story. A body found in the village. Tractors had been digging out the ditches and enlarging one of the ponds to take more water in the winter and reduce the issues with waterlogging and flooding at the lower end of the village. To their surprise, in stead of just dirt, a body had been lifted from the shallow water in the undergrowth. No formal identification yet, just a skeleton left but police had said it was probably ten to twenty years old. Sam-son of one of the right sort of villagers- had been there and seen the skeleton. He had come home and told his parents. His Father was now regaling the men outside with it. Indoors his wife was waiting for the opportunity to tell the story too, but the ladies were still politely discussing how beautiful the house now was.

As the clock turned to nine o clock, Sean carried out a box he had earlier placed in the larder and placed it beside her. Sam's mother inwardly sighed in frustration, clearly her hostess had something to show and her story would have to wait.

Pinging her wineglass with a handy teaspoon, she recalled all their attention to her and told them all that she had had little momento books printed for them all to look at and take away with them. Immediately the women started cooing and complimenting her on her forethought. Sean started giving them out and while the women were commenting on the first couple of pages, engrossed, she silently left the room with Claire, with the rest of her family following.

Chapter 34

'You want to leave me.' he said blankly, 'You plan to leave me, leave me here.' he said softly but with suppressed anger in his expression. Suddenly she felt nervous. Their pond was very remote, not visible at all from the footpath and no one was likely to be passing it anyway. Their blanket was laid a ten minute walk from the path, no one was likely to even hear them, sound was muffled by the thick

coverage of trees and brambles. Suddenly the very appeal of the area, made her feel vulnerable and she knew Gran would not have approved of her being alone in such a secluded spot with him.
He pulled her close and she felt herself flinch. The flash in his eyes told him she felt it too and wasn't happy. She no longer felt safe.
'I want you to come too.' She tried to reassure him, she could hear the tremble in her own voice and she knew he could hear it too. She sounded insincere, placating.
'You want to leave me.' he repeated, his voice becoming even quieter but somehow more threatening. His grasp on her became tighter and she realised how much stronger than her he was. His years of odd jobs, manual labour, gardening and cycling anywhere he had wanted to be had honed the muscles in his body. Whereas, her more pampered lifestyle had left her slim and weak. Fear flashed through her, she had put herself in a situation which could prove to be dangerous. But this was Jasper, her boyfriend, he wasn't dangerous... was he? Her mind flashed back to yesterday and today, his mum's bruises, her flinch as he came near her. It couldn't be, could it? The girl who tried to warn her...
She returned to the present, to see Jasper watching her closely, for a brief moment she worried he could read her mind, but her Catholic upbringing told her that was impossible. His eyes had narrowed slightly and his grip on her seemed to be growing even tighter. She felt trapped and frightened.
'Jasper, you're hurting me. Please let go.' She spoke with trepidation.
'You're leaving *me*. Like my dad left. You don't think I'm good enough. You let me kiss you and touch your breasts. *Fucking pricktease*. And now you *think* you can just leave me.'
'No Jasper, I want us to go together. Come with me. Gran will help you find a job and somewhere to work. You could do people's gardens or work in a library. There are loads of jobs in London. And loads of rooms to rent.'
His other hand held her other arm too now, painfully. 'You think your *darling* gran would let you date me. No university education, no family, no prosepects. She wouldn't help me!'
Before she could assure him that Gran would, he'd he pulled her against him and held her so she could barely breathe. He started kissing her. But this kiss wasn't like the others, it was fierce and hurt her. He bit her lips and she could taste the blood on her mouth where

he had broken the skin. She was very, very frightened.
She tried to pull back but his hands went to her neck and she was choking, as she struggled to breathe he started ripping at her clothes. His mouth was on her breast and it was painful. He was grasping at her, his mouth around her nipple, biting, and his hand squeezing so hard it hurt. She froze, unable to fight him off and scared of angering him further if she tried, still struggling for breath.
She realised she was praying, 'Hail Mary, full of grace, the lord is with thee...' Then 'Our Father, who art in Heaven...' In her mind she could feel her rosary beads between her fingers as she prayed.
She wasn't sure how long she was praying for trying not to feel him touching her.
Then his hands travelled lower, pulling at her jeans and working their way into her knickers. Her jeans were around her knees and she came back to reality squirming and screaming to try to stop him. His hand was pulling at her vulva trying to work its way into her vagina and she was screaming and begging him to stop, kicking at him and pushing him away.
He muttered angrily while he did these things. 'fucking bitch, pricktease. Getting what you deserve.'
Her ears barely registered the ongoing insults as she fought against him frutilessly.
Suddenly, he let go with one hand as he used that hand to undo his trousers and start sliding them down. This gave her the opportunity she needed and she jumped to her feet, managing to disengage his other hand.
He too jumped to his feet and grabbed at her...
While she was still on the blanket he had spread, he had stepped up onto the mud beside him. The rain the previous day and night had not sunk into the dry ground, leaving it slippery and he was struggling to keep his balance. As he reached out towards and tried to grab her, she pushed him away and he slipped falling backwards.
Without a backwards glance, she ran through the brambles cutting herself further. She ran to the footpath and kept running down the footpath back to the comparative safety of her Dad's house. All the way, she thought she could hear footsteps. She didn't even pause to do up her jeans, instead holding them as she ran. She took the back route up the footpath to her Dad's house. She didn't even notice the horse girls were not in the field.

Upon reaching the empty house, she locked all the doors and not even changing her clothes, closed herself in her bedroom, staring but unseeing.

Chapter 35

As the four cars drove back to London and away from James, the chaos they had unleashed on the unsuspecting friends and neighbours was slowly coming to fruition. At first, no one really realised almost a dozen people had left the party, assuming they had gone to hand out books or find seats elsewhere to look through the book. All the ladies in the kitchen were politely engrossed in 'The Story of Us', thinking it was a slightly over-romantic gesture, cooing appreciatively as they looked through the first few pages (although a couple of the ladies were slightly aghast at the age gap, a teenager and a man clearly in his thirties in the early photos). Then as the tone of the photos changed, with James drunk and then the photos of the e mails and her injuries, people started to look up and realise that she was no longer there, nor were the older couple or the younger couple, or the helpful young men, in fact all her friends had vanished...

Realising people were staring at her, Lisa turned the pages of the book to see her starring role in photos she really didn't want her husband or colleagues to see. Hurriedly, she stood up and rushed outside to convince her husband to leave. But too late she realised, a couple of wives were already outside with their husband, away from the barbecue gasping at the photos. More women were making their way outside to their husbands, books open, looking horrified.

Unaware of what was unfolding around them, James and a couple of others stood beside the barbecue chatting inconsequentially about sport and the chances of their favourite teams next season. Slowly, one by one, the husbands were called away by their wives and hushed whispers ensued.

As people started making their apologies and leaving, James suddenly became aware that something out of his control was occurring. What were the books everyone had in their hand and where was his wife with his next drink? It slowly dawned on him that people were looking at him with disgust instead of admiration. Lisa looked pale, even in this fading light...

Unsure quite what to do, he looked around as people were

leaving. A disgusted neighbour handed him a book as he left. He looked at the cover, nothing to be disgusted about there that he could see? Then he started looking through the pages, the fist few seems innocuous- a bit embarrassing maybe... then... Furious, he marched towards the house, he had to speak to her *now,* even if her friends were there. If she thought she could get away with this...

He didn't even register Lisa and his boss arguing, or her sobs as he stormed into the house. He looked everywhere, but he couldn't find her. Eventually, he registered her empty office, the lack of any books on the shelves and then her empty side of the walk-in wardrobe. He heard the front door slam and walked downstairs glancing out the window to see the final car driving away, leaving just his in the drive.

He knew where she would be, that house in London... he went for his car keys but they weren't in their normal place, where he remembered putting them earlier... Only then did he notice a sobbing Lisa standing watching him.

By now, the four cars were turning onto the M11, both sets of the keys to his new BMW sitting in Claire's Mother's capacious handbag. She already planned to bin them at the services near Stanstead, it would certainly make his life harder and hopefully stop him from coming to London tonight at least.

It was late when they eventually arrived back in London and the four cars pulled up outside her house. Claire's parents hugged her goodnight and left, back to their house, while the rest came in with her, to talk about the evening that had been.

Walking in, surrounded by family, she felt happier and less alone than she had since Gran had died.

Watching Sean pull two bottles of champagne from his car, she knew that she still had one piece of news to break to them...

Chapter 36

It was late evening when her Father and Sheryl reached home. She wasn't in her bedroom as they would have expected, she was crouched, sobbing against the kitchen door. Her hair was half loose from its ponytail. Her face had scratches and there was dried blood. Her top was ripped and the bruises around her neck and bite marks on her chest were visible. She sobbed silently, her body and mind

exhausted.
Her Father and Sheryl came into the house, and Sheryl went straight upstairs to bed. Her Father went into the kitchen to check the door was locked and came face to face with his daughter. She looked at him through eyes red from crying, bruised and bloody. Her jeans still unfastened. He stood and stared, his mouth open in shock.
Silently, they stared at each other, eventually, he spoke.
'You should be in bed. Looks like you need a shower too.' he said, ignoring all the obvious signs of attack. He looked away from her. 'Stop crying. Would you like to go back to your Gran a bit early, looks like you aren't too happy here...' He stopped for a moment. 'I can't take you tonight, but first thing in the morning. Go to bed now.' He put his hands on his hips and looked at her expectantly.

Still sobbing silently, she got to her feet, her head spinning and dropped the knife he hadn't noticed her clutching and slowly wended her way upstairs.

Pausing only to put the knife in the dishwasher, and shake his head in disbelief, he followed her muttering. 'Can't have Sheryl upset when she is carrying my son. Her gran will know what to do. Not fair to put that stress on Sheryl.'

The sounds of the shower followed and she went to bed to hear the usual nightly pleasures of her father and Sheryl which tonight seemed even harder to hear. She lay awake, her books untouched and rocked gently to try and comfort herself. Tomorrow she would be with Gran... Tomorrow she would be away from here and she would make sure she never came back. As night became day, she made sure the last of her things were packed and went downstairs ready to go home to Gran and all that was safe and comfortable. She sat by the door, ready and waiting for her father to come down.

It was after eight when he eventually came downstairs and she had been waiting for hours. She was still pale and some injuries were still visible. He flinched at the sight of her scratches and bruises, but didn't comment on them. He explained that he couldn't take the time to drive her, but there was a train soon, he'd drop her at the station and give her the train fare as a belated birthday present. He handed her thirty pounds.
They headed out to the car. Anybody watching would simply see a young teenager was sullenly getting into the back seat of an

expensive modern BMW seemingly oblivious to her surroundings, while a still-young-looking father got into the front with a look of relief. The boot held a couple of suitcases and anyone looking carefully would see that under the sunglasses, the girl's eyes were red rimmed. Without conversation, or even looking at each other, they departed.

Within fifteen minutes the BMW had returned to its neat driveway without the sullen teenager and a far more jaunty looking man than before climbed out of the car shouting cheery a greeting as he entered the house.

At the station, a couple of miles away, the sullen looking teenager sat on a station bench with her two suitcases, heavy for her to handle waiting for the train which wasn't due for another thirty minutes. Every time anyone entered the platform through the squeaky gate, she looked up, but her large sunglasses hid the fear in her eyes and most of the bruises and scratches on her face.

Epilogue

Six months later.

She sat at her kitchen table, her very new baby asleep in the old silver cross pram beside her. A pram which had been built to last and had once held her mother, then later her. She was listening to carols on the radio as she cut out biscuits, and she looked happy but tired.

The kitchen door opened and Claire came in, carrying her sleeping baby, her toddler by her side.

'Katharine, merry Christmas Eve's Eve!' she shouted as she came in the door laughing. She put her bag on the floor and a newspaper on the edge of the table, away from the biscuits.

Happily, Claire and Katharine chatted, as Claire finished off the biscuits for the party later, happy and comfortable together, carefree and excited for Christmas.

Had either of them read the newspaper, there were two very small articles which might have interested Katharine and one which might have interested Claire. But as they didn't even glance at the newspaper nothing disturbed their day.

One article merely announced that the body found earlier that year in a pond, in a village they both knew, had been identified as Jasper Jacobs. It had been concluded he had fallen and sustained a head injury, leading to him drowning so the case was now closed.

The other article alluded to a certain James being arrested for assault and being drunk and disorderly.

As neither of them glanced at the paper, which was later used for muddy boots, their minds stayed in the happiness of the present and the future.

Printed in Great Britain
by Amazon